THE SAT

"In *The Satchel and Other Terrors*, author Matias Travieso-Diaz takes the reader on an engrossing tour of the darkest corners of this world and others, the past, present, dark futures, and even other planes of conscience and reality. No matter how bizarre, strange, or twisted the story, Travieso-Diaz's living, breathing characters are the life's blood of the tale. 'Liebestod' is my personal favorite of the collection, but there's more than enough wonder and dread for any fan of horror or dark fantasy. A must-read for lovers of these genres."

~ Jason J. McCuiston, author of *Project Notebook* and
The Last Star Warden series

"Matias Travieso-Diaz takes you on a worldwide thrill-ride in this collection of creepy tales. He weaves macabre ideas with well-researched geographical and historical details. His stories remind readers the world can be a very scary place indeed. Best read from the comfort (and safety) of home!"

~ Adrian Ludens, author of *The Tension of a Coming Storm* and *Bottled Spirits & Other Dark Tales*

"Mr. Travieso-Diaz's short stories in *The Satchel and Other Terrors* are like the bloody news photograph that you know you should not look at, but click on anyway. However, there is more in them than the terrifying places to which he leads you with his elegant black pen, and towards which you continue to follow even after you realize how cruel they are, like Old World fairy tales. There is a great diversity of time and geography in them, narratives that turn and then turn again with surprise, and exotic characters who gradually become familiar because they plumb archetypes moved by fear, greed, and love. More importantly, Mr. Travieso-

Diaz leads you to the realization that terror begins in the familiar places, the hearth, the school, and the office, metastasizes into the terrors that haunt us collectively, and transforms banal, complacent souls into monsters."

~ Alex Ferrate

"Using a passel of classic story formats, Matias Travieso-Diaz has given us nineteen delightfully varied macabre, grotesque or somewhat perverse tales. He delights in diverse artistic forms, indicating his inspiration with a quote at the top of each story. His influences range from fairy tales to operatic standards, from folk legends to literary myths. There is no shortage of psychological overtones to these stories.

"The reader will enjoy Travieso-Diaz's wide-ranging knowledge, reflected in the subject matters of these tales. If you like Faustian bargains, there's a story for you. If your taste runs to Dantean Purgatory, you'll find something to please. Readers who seek ethnic and historic scope, with a large dose of the gruesome, will no doubt be satisfied. Some tales are definitely morbid, some merely ending in an ironic twist. There is a grim tale for everyone!"

~ Roxanne Greenstein

"Matias uses the tone and feel of age-old tales to illustrate the distorting, often tragic effects of human weakness. With a nod to Poe, Grimm, O. Henry, and even Stephen King, the author holds up human greed, jealousy, bloodlust, avarice, fear, bigotry, and other 'deadly sins' to a kind of funhouse mirror and reveals how much the distortion we see reflected back is more realistic than we might care to admit. Though often set in some faraway land or undetermined, mythical past, these stories reverberate with an anxiety and spiritual unease that very much speak to today's world. The author has tucked a burr in our souls and left us itching and squirming. And that is as it should be."

~ Stephen Kimmerling

"The imagination, wide diversity of stories, and surprise endings are what make *The Satchel and Other Terrors* by Matias Travieso-Diaz such a delight to read. The imagination that Matias brings to us through his stories is a treasure worth savoring. I find the storylines for 'Slug' and 'Dummies' to be mind boggling. Where in the world did Matias come up with the ideas for these imaginative tales? I have never read anything like them. There are many other similarly imaginative and unique tales to be found in *The Satchel and Other Terrors*. Matias's imaginative stories never cease to amaze me.

"And the stories cover a wide range of themes in diverse settings. Stories of death, revenge, greed, mystery, fantasy, criminal investigation, science fiction in settings of every stripe. Stories in the past, the future, the afterlife, the wild west, medieval ages, as well as pure fantasy. It is impossible to become bored reading tales of such imagination and wide ranging storylines and settings.

"Finally, one never knows how the stories will end. The reader is captured in suspense. What is going to happen? How is this going to end? One of my favorites is 'Rosalba.' The reader will never guess the ending of this story revealed only in the last paragraph of three sentences. Similarly, nearly all the other tales have endings that will escape the reader until virtually the end of the story.

"So, *The Satchel and Other Terrors* is a treat for all readers, the young, the old, the fun loving, and the serious. Everyone should find something to love in these imaginative, wildly diverse, and suspenseful tales."

~ Paul Gaukler

THE SATCHEL
AND OTHER TERRORS

BY

MATIAS TRAVIESO-DIAZ

Cover art and design by The Busy Dee
instagram.com/thebusydee

Visit us on our website at:
www.darkowlpublishing.com

ALSO FROM
DARK OWL PUBLISHING

Collections

The Dark Walk Forward
John S. McFarland

*The Last Star Warden
Volumes I and II*
Jason J. McCuiston

*The Last Star Warden:
The Phantom World*
Jason J. McCuiston
Available on Kindle Vella

*No Lesser Angels, No Greater
Devils*
Laura J. Campbell

*The Tension of a Coming
Storm*
Adrian Ludens

The Nightmare Cycle
Lawrence Dagstine
Coming April 2023

The Art of Ghost Writing
Alistair Rey
Coming June 2023

*The Brotherhood of Secret
Darkness and Other Cults,
Cabals, and Conspiracies*
Jason J. McCuiston
Coming June 2023

Anthologies

*A Celebration of Storytelling
Something Wicked This Way
Rides*

Novels

The Black Garden
John S. McFarland

The Mother of Centuries
The sequel to *The Black
Garden*
John S. McFarland

The Keeper of Tales
Jonathon Mast

Just About Anyone
Carl R. Jennings

The Malakiad
Gustavo Bondoni

Carnivore Keepers
Kevin M. Folliard

The Wicked Twisted Road
D.S. Hamilton

TABLE OF CONTENTS

THE SATCHEL

There are two types of people in this world. People who hate clowns... and clowns.
- D. J. MacHale

We have to be careful when we walk in the open. There are always bad people on the lookout for the likes of us, and if they catch us (as happened once, not long ago) there will be loud insults, kicking and punching, or worse.

The kids have been told to be wary of us, for we will try to lure them away for some evil purpose. They must run, and they must warn their elders so they can pursue us, cudgels and pitchforks at the ready. We are only safe by dropping back into the forest or reaching the foot of the mountain where there are sheltering caves. We need to avoid being seen during the day and only venture out at night to forage in the fields, catching small animals or plucking fruit from trees, and sometimes stealing eggs from henhouses. It is a miserable and dangerous life, made necessary by our own deeds and the cruelty of men.

It was not always like this. Before, I could stroll among crowds, hardly drawing attention from anyone. But of late I needed to start wearing gloves and had to make a rough covering for my face out of thick canvas. We tried to make it more human-looking by stealing dyes from the tannery and turning the piece into a white oval over which we painted large smiling red lips, black eyes set below black eyebrows, and an orange ball for a nose. As my overflowing dark hair shot out behind and around the mask, the composite became the face of a jester—and not a good-looking one.

Reflected in a rain puddle, the image of the mask was terrifying. We had a sudden impulse to throw it away and start all over again. But there was no guarantee that a new mask would be less hideous, and at any rate, the mask was intended to conceal, not display my true self.

Now winter was approaching and living off the land was getting increasingly difficult, so we had to move south to milder lands. A pass through the mountains was guarded by border patrols of two nations, but we managed to elude them in the dead of night, thanks to a violent storm that had the guards abandon their stations in search of shelter. The trip through the highlands past the border was very difficult, with the cold winds cutting through our garments and food turning from scarce to non-existent. We nearly froze or starved to death until, by the grace of God, the last mountain pass was surmounted and the land dropped gently to a region that was much warmer and where grasses grew and some fruits still hung from trees. We rushed down to find a respite from the cold and sample what the land had to offer; fish were found in abundance in gentle rivers, and field mice and squirrels were available for trapping and eating raw, for we hate fire and will eat nothing that requires us to cook with it.

A few days after reaching the warmer region, we came to a hamlet where people seemed less violent than those across the mountains. We spied on the local inhabitants for a few days before deciding that it might be safe to approach them. Late one afternoon, as the sun started to drop behind the hills, we slowly moved toward a hut that was set apart from the others and waved hello to an old man who sat on a bench at the hut's entrance. He was taken aback by our appearance, including the dirty rags that barely covered my body, the filthy cape, the large pilgrim satchel slung over one shoulder, the beard that protruded from below the mask, the frizzy hair, the gloves, and the mask itself. Even though startled, the old man waved back hello and made a summoning sign with his arm, inviting us—me and the satchel—to come closer.

Reluctantly, we did, even though friendly gestures are rare and need to be received with suspicion. The man began talking in an unknown language, but seeing that I did not understand, he mimicked a question. He rubbed his stomach and then pointed at us, asking if we were hungry. I nodded vigorously. The man got up, opened the hut's door, and beckoned us to follow.

Inside, it was all very rustic: plain wood table and chairs, earthenware pots and dishes, wildflowers in a blue glazed vase. There were framed religious prints on the walls and a small bookcase with dusty books on half-empty shelves. A faded yellow curtain at the back of the room seemed to lead to other rooms. On the stove, a pot of cooked polenta was slowly cooling. An old woman was bent over the counter adding butter to a saucepan containing sautéed mushrooms. A jug of wine sat next to the saucepan.

The old man grabbed my arm and led us to the table. The woman took four wooden bowls out of a cupboard and ladled the semi-solid polenta into each of them. She set the bowls on the table, spooned the mushrooms over the polenta, and added grated cheese to each bowl. She did all of these with practiced ease, as the man filled glasses with wine.

I was focusing on the feast about to be served and did not notice that the back curtain had parted and a young girl, no more than sixteen, had entered the room and approached the table. She uttered a piercing scream when she saw us and cowered, covering her face with her hands.

The old man and the woman rushed to the girl, seeking to calm her down. We became afraid of what might follow and took advantage of the momentary confusion to pick up a bowl, run to the front door, and disappear into the evening. Once a good distance away from the hut, I savored the polenta, my first real meal in months. But we missed the warmth of human interaction, no longer to be had.

That night we sneaked into a sheep barn and, skirting the mildly protesting animals, found a quiet corner to catch a few hours of sleep. Early the next morning before daybreak, I stole a young lamb, to be devoured later, and ran away into the still-darkened countryside as dogs started to bark their threats.

It took only a few days to determine that the people of the south were no different from those beyond the mountains. A few folks caught glimpses of us as we roamed the fields and invariably shook their fists or made the sign of the cross. Once we had to run away, pursued by a rainstorm of rocks.

After two months of fugitive life in this foreign land, we could not stand it any longer. We came upon a village and headed for the church, which was recognizable as the only building with more than one story. The wooden doors were closed, as it was well into the night. I pounded on them, demanding admittance. After a few minutes, a disheveled priest in a night robe opened the door part way and inquired:

"What brings you here at this late hour?"

"Father, I need to have you hear my confession."

"Can't it wait until the morning?"

"Please, Father, I must unburden myself!"

The priest sighed and opened the door. "Come and sit for a few minutes while I get dressed."

A little later, I was kneeling at the confessional. "Bless me, Father, for I have sinned," I said.

"How long has it been since your last confession?"

"One and a half years, Father."

"What are your sins?"

"My sins are many, but I would start with the most serious ones. I have killed or caused the death of several people."

There was an audible gasp. "How did you do this?"

"My wife Coralina and I were mimes, traveling with a circus. Another mime, Domino, was also part of our act. Coralina gave birth to a beautiful girl with whom I fell in love right away. The afternoon of the child's first birthday, our circus was pitched on a clearing some distance away from a small town. Coralina asked me to go to the village to buy a torte and other goods to celebrate the occasion. I was halfway out on the route to town when I discovered that I had left the purse with my money behind. On returning to our tent to retrieve it, I heard noises inside which were clearly the sounds of lovemaking. I did not need to go in to learn that my wife and Domino were having intimate relations.

"I was seething with rage but restrained myself, partly because of deep shame at having to acknowledge Coralina's deception and also because Domino is much bigger than I and could hurt me badly if it came to a fight. I retreated to the ringmaster's tent and asked him to lend me some money, which I promised to repay before the day was out. The ringmaster was surprised by my request but gave me a few coins. So, I left for the village again, as a plot to avenge myself started to take shape in my head.

"My first stop was at the town chemist. I complained to him that I was having trouble getting to sleep and was looking for something strong to help me get the rest I needed. The chemist said this was a common affliction and the best cure he knew of was valerian, which had been used for centuries to treat insomnia. He produced a copper tin full of brownish shavings of different sizes. 'This is ground valerian root, the best sleep-inducing agent,' he said. 'You can use it to make tea; a couple of cups of valerian root tea will put you to sleep in minutes. But beware: it has an unpleasant taste, like that of weeds mixed with dirt. I recommend that you add a lot of honey to the brew to mask the bad taste. As an alternative, you can use alcohol in any form, like wine, to dissolve the root slivers and disguise their flavor.'

"I thanked him and bought a pouch of the ground root. I then went to the wine merchant, from whom I bought a bottle of coarse red wine and a large flask. After leaving his shop, I emptied the entire pouch into the flask, filled it almost to the top with wine, and shook it thoroughly so that the ground root would dissolve. I took a small sip of the mixture; it tasted off, but one could think it was just the poor quality of the wine. I completed other purchases and returned to the circus as night was falling.

"That night Coralina, Domino, and I had a modest feast with chicken, cold meats, fruits, and the birthday torte. As she served the dessert, I poured two generous cups of wine and handed them out. I gave myself a cup also, but only pretended to drink it. Coralina made a face when she first sipped the wine, but before she could protest, I explained, 'It is wine from the foot of the Atlas Mountains. It takes a bit to get used to the taste, but believe me, it is quite good.'

"Domino let out a great guffaw and said, 'It tastes like the cheap wine it is, but I like it,' and proceeded to drain his cup and presented it to me for a refill.

"Less than an hour later, the valerian had done its work. Domino was hunched over the table, snoring loudly. My wife had managed to stay sitting on her chair, her head sunk on her chest, also snoring.

"I took from my pilgrim satchel several lengths of rope that were part of the day's purchases and tied Domino's legs to his chair, and Coralina's to hers. The ropes would slow the lovers down for at least a few critical moments.

"I then glanced at the crib, where the baby lay quietly. What was I going to do with her? She was for sure Domino's child, not mine. All of a sudden, I hated her. Should she be spared? The answer was no.

"I proceeded to the last step in my revenge. I tore a sheet into pieces, soaked each piece in cooking oil, and set each on fire, tossing them into all corners of the tent, and ran out for safety as the flimsy structure started to go up in flames. I was only out a few steps when I heard the loud wail of a baby in distress. I had a sudden pang of conscience, rushed back into the burning tent, found her bellowing with her clothes on fire, and rushed out with her in my arms, screaming as the fire licked into my face and hands.

"Inside, Domino and Coralina had woken up. They tried

to free themselves as the flames closed in on them. They failed, and their desperate screams resonated in the silence of the night. Help rushed in from the other tents, but the rescuers arrived too late.

"I ran until I reached the woods that surrounded the village. There I made a stop to rest for a moment. For the first time, I noticed that I was in great pain from burns over the exposed areas of my body. Turning to the child I held against my chest, I made another discovery: she was not breathing. I shook her tiny body, pinched her cheeks, tried to breathe life into her mouth. She was dead. I have no idea how, but she had perished in my arms, and it was all my fault.

"When my mind cleared somewhat from the pangs of pain and grief, I realized that I was the prime suspect for the deaths of Domino and Coralina, and it would not be long before they started chasing after me with riders and hunting dogs. So, we ran further into the wilderness. In time, I made this mask to cover my burned face, put on gloves to hide the burns on my hands, and went into hiding, always carrying with me the remains of my daughter. See?"

I opened the pilgrim satchel. Immediately, an intolerable stench of decay filled the small church. Peering inside, the priest saw a clutch of small bones, some with shreds of rotting meat attached to them. He convulsed and retched. After a while, he recovered enough to continue administering the sacrament.

"Your sins are grievous and call for retribution from God as well as man. You should surrender yourself to the authorities and abide by their judgment. As for—"

I interrupted, "But Father, my crimes were committed in another country. Justice would not be served if I am punished here."

The priest continued. "What to do about the justice of men is between them and you. As for the mercy of God, you must perform a very demanding act of penitence."

"Like what?"

"Half an hour down the road that goes east out of town

is a holding encircled by a tall fence. The fence has an entrance with a gate and a sign that reads *House of Lazarus*. You must go to that gate and ring its bell, seeking admittance. When they come in response to the bell, tell them that you want to serve the community. They will let you in."

"What kind of a place is it?"

"A leper colony. What we call a lazar house."

"What if I refuse to go?"

"God will not grant you absolution for your grave sins without the required penitence."

I motioned towards the satchel and we rose as if to leave. The priest watched as the satchel closed. He added, "And since this confession has not been completed and your sins have not been forgiven, I will feel obliged to tell the town's constable what you have told me and let him decide what to do with you."

I thought the priest was bluffing and considered wringing his scrawny neck and bolting out of this accursed village. But we were tired. Very tired. So, I replied, "Very well. I will go to the House of Lazarus."

The priest's face broke into a wan smile and, raising his right hand, he intoned: "*Ego te absolvo a peccatis tuis in nomine Patris, et Filii, et Spiritus Sancti. Amen.* Go in peace and sin no more."

So it was that, as night gave way to dawn, the satchel and I found ourselves at the gate of the House of Lazarus. The bell, as I swung it, rang with great force, filling the morning with metallic echoes. There was a long silence, and I was about to swing the cord again when slow steps sounded as an attendant approached the gate.

"How can we assist you, brother?" said the attendant, a wizened small man who seemed bent with age and fatigue.

"I have come to serve the community," was my response, as directed.

The old man sighed and produced an iron key, but before inserting it into the lock he demanded, "You must remove your mask before entering this place. Here nothing can be hidden, for the worst deformities of the lepers have to be observed and accepted without shame as God's will."

Those words seemed to lift a heavy burden that had been weighing on my soul for months. I removed the clownish mask and let the morning breeze caress my scarred face. As the key turned into the lock and the gate slowly opened, I dropped the satchel in the woods behind me and walked in, seeking redemption.

"What was that?" asked the gatekeeper, noticing how I had discarded the satchel.

"Nothing much. The bones of a young lamb that I consumed a while back."

SLUG

*Slugs crawl and crawl over our cabbages, like the world's
slander over a good name.
You may kill them, it is true; but there is the slime.*
- Douglas William Jerrold

*One morning, as Gregor Samsa was waking up from anx-
ious dreams, he discovered that in bed he had been
changed into a monstrous verminous bug.*
- Franz Kafka, *Metamorphosis*

Arun was an untouchable (or as they say nowadays, a
davit), a human being at the very bottom of the Indian caste system—indeed, beneath all castes. He
was born in the countryside in the Bastar district of
the Indian State of Chhattisgarh. Bastar is notorious for the
poverty and backwardness of its rural citizens. The Bastar
untouchables are the lowest of the low, barely a step above
the beasts in the field.

Arun never knew his father, and his mother ran away,
abandoning him shortly after birth. His maternal grandmother took pity on the baby and rescued him from certain
death. She brought Arun to her hovel in the city of Jagdalpur and took care of him through his early years.

It was not only the shame of having given birth to a bastard that drove Arun's mother to run away. The newborn
was found to have a fluid-filled sac in the middle of his
back, covered by a thin layer of skin. Arun's mother be-
lieved that the boy had been set upon at birth by a *Dasyu*,

an evil demon that would eventually destroy him and bring ruin to his kin.

She was only partially wrong, for Arun was not a normal child. He suffered from weakness of the muscles of his legs and had trouble walking, a deficiency that increased as he grew older so that he could only move around using crutches. There were other problems: he had a curved spine and one of his hips hung lower than the other; he could not control his bladder or his bowels and was frequently soiling himself; he lacked sensation in his feet, legs, and buttocks, and did not notice when he got wounds, blisters, or sores. In short, he was a poor physical specimen.

Arun's grandmother tended to him the best she could but was too poor to get him medical attention. Sending Arun to school was also out of the question. Thus, from an early age, he was limited to begging for alms outside his tenement, under his grandmother's watchful eye. He taught himself to play the *bansuri* (a side-blown bamboo flute) and wove plaintive melodies to attract donors.

Even though he played the *bansuri* well and begged diligently, Arun had little success in his work. As a *davit*, he was considered so impure that people of other castes were affronted by the mere sight of him. His frequent wetting and soiling himself aggravated the negative reactions, and passers-by often crossed to the other side of the street to avert him and walked quickly away. So the alms he gathered were few and far between and were often prompted by the people's sense of shame at feeling such revulsion for another human being, no matter how debased.

Through some miracle, Arun survived until his grandmother died, shortly after he turned sixteen. He was left alone sitting on the street outside the tenement where he once lived, wasting away and covered in his own filth. He would have starved to death had he not been spotted by a policeman, who determined that Arun was a public nuisance and needed to be removed from the eyes of the citizenry. He sought to make arrangements for the youth to be transported to a Christian-run community health center, where he was to be cared for by nuns and lay volunteers.

Two young men were conscripted to carry Arun to the health center on a stretcher. They were dark-skinned Sudras, members of one of the lowest Indian castes. They had to reluctantly obey the orders of the policeman, who was a higher-caste Kshatriya. Each man was given a few coins as recompense for the task of taking Arun since the boy was regarded as so polluted that touching or being near him was to be avoided.

The trip started without incident, but as they were marching on a trail by a drainage canal, the man at the front got a foot caught on a rut in the road and fell to his knees. The stretcher overturned, and Arun tumbled to the ground. Unfortunately, his bowels chose that moment to discharge, covering him and the stretcher in foul-smelling excrement.

The Sudras were disgusted. One asked the other, "What now? We can't pick him up without contaminating ourselves, and the stretcher is soiled with his shit. Should we just abandon him here?"

"We can't do that," replied the other. "People walking on this road will eventually find him, and the police may trace him back to us."

"Then what do we do?"

Their conversation was interrupted by Arun, who tried to sit, fell back, and lay spread-eagled on the ground. Although speaking was difficult for him, he managed to implore in a low guttural voice, "Please, don't leave me here. I'll soon die if am not given help." He then burst into tears.

"Shut up!" cried one of the men. "You have dirtied us enough already!"

"I have an idea," said the other. "Let's dump him in the canal. From here, it flows into the River Indrawati, so the body may never be found or may come ashore leagues from here."

"But then we have to carry him to the canal. I don't want to touch his filthy body."

"We'll just push him to the edge of the water and dump him in with a branch or something."

"Sounds good. What are we going to tell the police?"

"We'll say that we delivered him to the nuns and left him in their care. I don't think the police will follow up."

Arun listened to the men's exchange with horror and began whimpering and shaking convulsively. "Please, no. Please, don't do it. For the love of Krishna, I beg you. Just leave me alone!" His olive skin had turned ghostly white, and his breathing had become labored.

One of the young men gave the prone figure a savage kick. "Shut up! You are dead already, you piece of dung!"

Arun uttered a loud cry, and his body went limp. He had passed out.

His fainting was, in a way, mercy, for he did not witness the series of vicious kicks with which the men moved his body to the canal's edge. It was hard, brutal work, and by the time they had Arun by the water, they were drenched in sweat. Both of them had cut branches from trees growing by the road and used them to shove Arun's body into the murky waters. He dropped in and sank.

"Let's go," said one. "We'll need to take a purification bath right away," said the other. They left without looking back.

* * *

When Arun regained consciousness a few moments later, he was floating on his back in the dirty waters of the canal. His body hurt as if every bone had been crushed. He had trouble breathing, and his vision was blurred. He was only able to make small motions that drew him slowly toward the shore. After what seemed an eternity, he found himself hanging from a shrub at the water's edge. Carefully, he lowered himself to the bottom and noticed that he could stand as the water only reached his chest. He realized he might not be able to get out unaided and was again seized by despair. He was exhausted, broken, and surprisingly hungry. He wished for death to come to end his agony, recalling the Hindu teaching he had received from his grandmother:

When he died, his soul would be reborn in a different body, hopefully much improved over his current one.

Yet some force made him rebel against untimely death. He wanted to survive, get justice, mete out retribution against those two men and all others who had wronged him in his short life. He held onto the shrub with all his might but soon fell into a waking trance.

On the road near the edge of the canal, he then saw an odd animal: a very large olive-brown creature with a moist, elongated body that lay flat on the ground. It was legless and had two pairs of long tentacles protruding from the head followed by a saddle-shaped structure and a long tail. It moved by contracting and releasing the muscles on the underside of the body while at the same time secreting a sticky mucus as it traveled. It looked like a snail without a shell, and it seemed harmless despite its odd appearance.

As he gazed at the animal, Arun felt a sense of communion with the visitor, and then a strange desire to be like it. After a while, he started to experience the same sensations as the slug. He could see and smell through the top pair of tentacles, touch and taste through the lower pair. He drew air through an opening on the saddle behind its head and felt an increasing hunger for anything vegetable: leaves, fruits, mushrooms, the lichen that coated the rocks by the canal—even the moss on the trees. He also perceived other, more complex emotions: a yearning for moisture, the fear of attack by predators, sexual longings. Arun could not totally mesh his human emotions with the primitive urges of the slug, but both sets of feelings coexisted and were mutually acknowledged. He came to feel that he was not just himself anymore but had become one with the beast. Little by little, he realized that he was able to experience the sense of being in the particular form of the slug while not actually changing physically.

He developed a sense of admiration for the slug's ability to be in harmony with its environment. With a pang of envy, he was awed by the creature's intactness, the absence of hurts, deformities, or feelings of inadequacy. The slug was strong and could take care of itself.

With a mighty effort, Arun propped himself up further so he was braced against the sand at the edge of the canal. The slug began moving away slowly, heading in the general direction of the nearby town, all the time feasting on the various forms of plant life, which he chomped through thousands of tiny teeth. Arun was too weak to get himself out of the canal, so he hung there, half of his body immersed in the fetid water as he watched his other self slither away. But the psychic link between the two persisted: Arun could experience, without actually physically perceiving, the slug's sensations as it drew farther apart from him.

As the day warmed up and the slug inched away from the humid vicinity of the canal, its body, made mostly of water, began to dry up uncomfortably. It released mucus to keep itself moist but ultimately had to hide under a large fallen tree where it found dampness and shelter from the heat of the sun. It rested there, waiting for the night and yearning for rain.

* * *

The following day, heavy rains began, ushering in the start of the monsoon season. The slug shook itself into action and resumed its slow progress toward Jagdalpur as directed by the boy's mental urgings. Its progress took them by several of the many farms that dotted the Bastar district. The Zaid crops—pumpkin, cucumber, and gourds—were ripening and almost ready to be harvested.

The slug made frequent detours to sample the delicacies. It was going through a pumpkin patch, savoring the green and yellow fruits that lay on the ground, when a bark sounded and a large mangy dog approached, bent on mayhem.

Although far away, Arun blanched and cowered in fear, for the memory of the violent attack by the Sudras was still fresh in his mind. The slug, however, seemed prepared for the eventuality. It contracted its body, making itself more like a ball, and firmly attached itself to the ground, while at the same time releasing copious amounts of mucus. The dog tried in vain to get a firm hold of the slippery beast and, after several unsuccessful attempts at dislodging it, walked away from the slug, uttering a disconcerted growl.

It was at this point that Arun realized why the slug was his animal kintype. They were both ungainly, soft, and vulnerable, and both were despised and subject to attack by the hostile world. They differed only in that the slug had developed mechanisms for coping with those attacks—he had no such defenses.

* * *

The slug's crawling brought it in the early morning to the slums that ringed Jagdalpur, a succession of poorly built hovels with thatched roofs, crowded together randomly without sanitary or drinking water facilities. The slug proceeded slowly on the dirt road, oblivious to the human misery around it. Its first inkling of danger was the appearance of a pack of children ranging from toddlers to near teenagers. They were uniformly dirty, and most were naked. They noticed the slug with bored eyes, but then their expressions turned to malice as one of them picked a pebble from the road and threw it at the beast. It hit the slug with a plop and buried itself on its mantle before a convulsion from the slug succeeded in dislodging it.

Arun warned the slug to slink away from the children as fast as it could, and it began doing so, but one of the oldest in the group seized a large rock and hurled it at the animal, pinning it to the ground. Arun felt a sensation of excruciating pain and blacked out.

When he came to, the children had gone away. The slug had flattened and elongated its body until it was just a thin ribbon and was slowly crawling away from the rock under which it was buried. Arun could feel the intense pain experienced by the slug and its blind determination to escape its predicament and urged it on. Finally, the slug resumed moving on the dirt road, leaving a pale blue trail of blood in its wake.

After a few minutes, the slug detected a bramble bush by the side of the road and slid under it. Arun could feel its exhaustion as the animal's body reacted to the loss of fluids from the attack and the day's rising temperature. "We are dying," he observed with resignation.

Providentially, the afternoon's monsoon rains provided an injection of moisture to the ravaged body of the slug. It lay there, hiding and feeding on the brambles and recovering its strength for two days and nights. All the while, Arun felt himself near death and pondered what he should direct the slug to do next. His heart was heavy with sorrow and increasing anger at the callousness of his fellow humans. Somehow, his emotion managed to break through the barrier between species and resonated as a visceral dark feeling in the slug.

* * *

Arun had no particular destination in mind when he had steered the slug toward Jagdalpur; he was merely returning to the only place on earth he knew. However, as the slug reached town, its vision focused on a tall tower crowned by a large metal sphere; the tower was surrounded by a beehive of indigent shacks and tents. Arun realized that the tank stored water for the city, and a sudden dark thought occurred to him. Neither he nor the slug had any weapons they could use, but within the slug's body were thousands of larvae of a roundworm parasite whose presence Arun had detected as a generalized internal itch on the beast. Prompted by Arun, the slug could perhaps manage to get inside the tank, drop into the water, and drown. As it decomposed, the larvae it hosted would be released into the water, infecting it. Arun was no scientist, but he was smart enough to expect that the befouled water would be consumed by many, causing at least distress and potentially worse consequences. That would be at least some revenge for both him and the beast.

The ascent toward the spherical tank on top of the tower proved difficult because a slug's method of locomotion is not adapted for climbing. It proceeded by wrapping its soft, boneless body on one of the spindly legs of the tower and hoisting itself little by little. As the rain continued unabated, the slug did not dry out or overheat.

Finally, the slug was at the base of the tank, and Arun started to wonder how to get inside. The slug circled around the massive metal structure and discovered that there was a long narrow crack, like a spider web strand, running across the bottom of the tank. It would be fairly easy for the slug to enlarge the crack and squeeze through the opening. The slug had no hands or tools, but it started secreting a special form of highly acidic mucus that it often used to fight off predators. The slug attached itself to the base and began bathing the crack with corrosive slime. Midway through the intrusion, however, the enlarged crack began to leak: a trickle that could become a flood.

Arun then had a moment of self-reflection. His revenge was almost accomplished; soon, the slug would be able to squeeze into the tank and, dying, release its toxic innards into the water. However, there could be a massive outrush from the tank upon the ground below, reaching the shantytown that circled the tower; people might be hurt or drown. Did he have the right to hurt those innocent people? Conflicting emotions paralyzed his will. Should he direct the slug not to enter the tank but instead to provide an improvised patch that sealed the crack?

In the end, the thirst for retribution prevailed. Prompted by Arun, the slug dropped into the water and drowned. As it decomposed, the larvae it hosted were released into the water. The trickle of water exiting the tank continued but never became a flood.

Several weeks later, a pump failure in the municipal water system resulted in the flushing of the tower's water into Jagdalpur's potable water supply. Many cases of angiostrongyliasis, also known as rat lungworm, were later reported in the city; scores of people came down with bacterial meningitis, leading to paralysis and in many cases, death.

Arun did not survive to witness the result of his experiment, for he had died by the canal just as the slug drowned in the tank. Had he still lived, he would have rejoiced in his revenge.

A Very Cold Hand

Che gelida manina! Se la lasci riscaldar...
- Giacomo Puccini, "La Bohème," Act I

Rudolph, her husband of forty years, had just passed away, and Lucia was not in good health, so she decided to spend whatever time she had left traveling around the world. She researched the offerings of various cruise companies, the availability of overseas medical insurance (a must), internet access, and other potential cost items. She selected a company that offered budget Mediterranean cruises. She took the plunge and signed up for her first trip.

The cruise ship, somewhat ominously, was called *Olandezul Plutitoare,* which was translated by her owners as *The Cruising Dutchman*. The *Olandezul* sailed from Venice one cool afternoon in March with Lucia on board, bound for ports in Croatia and Montenegro on the Adriatic, on the way to Athens.

Lucia was disappointed at her lower deck, inside cabin, only large enough for a single bed, a desk with a chest of drawers, and an armchair. Closet space was, however, adequate, and she supplemented it with an over-the-door organizer. This allowed her to put away the numerous items she had chosen to bring onboard, including formal and casual wear, several pairs of shoes, and a large supply of cosmetics and health and beauty aids. She was planning to proceed from this tour to the next one upon returning to Venice.

On her desk she found a newsletter with details of the options for that evening and the following day. It was too late for the formal afternoon tea, but she could choose between set-seating dinner and no-set dining, that is, being placed at the first available table. She selected the latter, hoping to start making friends from that first day.

The dining room featured a buffet, with all sorts of tantalizing delicacies on display. Lucia decided to eat sparingly, for gaining weight during cruises was a well-known hazard she intended to avoid. A bit of Caesar salad, some fish and seafood, a dinner roll, and a cup of vichyssoise were all she brought to her table.

There were four people already there, three women and a man, all in their sixties or seventies, talking in low voices to each other. They paid no attention to Lucia, who greeted everyone warmly as she sat down. Other than a slight bowing of some heads, her arrival was unacknowledged.

Lucia frowned but put on her friendliest face and, turning to the lady on her left, attempted to break the ice by inquiring, "Is this your first Mediterranean cruise?" The lady clearly heard her but made no response. Lucia waited a second or two, and added, "It is my first. I'm hoping to take a walking tour of Athens when we get there." Again, no response.

Her attempts at conversation were put on hold by the arrival of a waiter, who was holding two open bottles of wine, one white and the other red. He approached Lucia, and motioned for her to make a choice. She pointed to the bottle of white wine and said, "Thanks, I will have some white wine. What kind are you serving?"

The waiter poured Lucia a generous glass and responded: "Pinot grigio." With that, he turned around and headed for the kitchen.

Lucia made a big show of picking the wine glass up and slightly flicking her wrist, making little circles in the air, then smelling into the glass and taking a sip. She commented to the table, "Ahh... I smell pineapple and lemons... it's a refreshing young wine." She did not know much about wine, but had taken a course at the adult center and had picked up the basic terms.

All her efforts to impress the audience and start a conversation failed to elicit even a nod of assent. Her companions were clearly ignoring her. Lucia was so flustered that she downed the wine in two big gulps, ate a morsel of salad, and got up abruptly, almost knocking her chair over.

"I've never been so humiliated in my life," she told herself, her cheeks still burning.

In her room, she tried to make sense of what had happened. "Did I say something wrong? Was I wearing too much perfume? Or maybe I should have put on better clothes, instead of jeans and a blouse?" She ran through and rejected many possibilities. Confused and dejected, she went to bed early, starting to feel pangs of hunger and longing for the abandoned meal.

The following morning, she got up early and had a satisfying breakfast alone in the empty dining room. She showered and got dressed in a casual but not too casual outfit. Overnight the ship had moored in Split, the largest city of Dalmatia. Split was ancient, its origins dating back to before the days of the Roman Empire. Lucia had read that the city had a number of points of interest, so she slipped away from the ship and inserted herself in a half-day excursion about to take off at the pier. The tour had an assigned guide; she took the tourists on a visit to Diocletian's Palace, once a huge palace of a Roman Emperor and now a beehive of shops, residences and cafés. The tour then went on by bus to Trogir, a small town near Split that had a medieval core surrounded by walls, a preserved castle and tower, and dwellings and palaces from the Romanesque, Gothic, Renaissance, and Baroque periods.

Throughout the tour, which started in the morning and ended in the late afternoon, the guide made many interesting announcements in good English but gave no answers to Lucia's questions, leaving her with the impression that either the guide's English was limited or she had broken some taboo that made her unwelcome. For that reason, the tour was not as pleasant as it could have been.

Lucia rushed back to the *Olandezul,* arriving near the end of the formal tea service. She found herself a love seat in the back of the room (which by that time was nearly empty) and waited to be served. Soon, a young girl arrived with a three-layer cake stand heaping with scones, candied fruits, petit-fours, and finger sandwiches. She placed the stand on a low table next to Lucia's seat and left, returning in a short while with an open box full of tea bags of many varieties. She presented the box to Lucia, indicating that she should choose some tea to her liking. Lucia perused the offerings and asked, "Do you have blackcurrant tea?"

A brief grimace of panic registered in the server's features. Swallowing hard, she replied in a very low voice, "No, ma'am."

Lucia frowned. She had expected the young girl to make a counteroffer, perhaps suggest wild berry or even blueberry, but she had said nothing. Irritated, Lucia inquired sharply, "Well, what do you recommend?" The girl turned around and ran away.

A while later, a sullen waiter in a cruise line uniform came over to Lucia holding a large teapot. As he poured silently into Lucia's cup, she recognized the dark hue of her favorite tea, blackcurrant.

Lucia could not stand it anymore. As the man finished pouring, Lucia asked in a loud voice that was almost a scream, "What's going on here? How come none of you people will talk to me or answer my questions?"

The man's face registered the fixed stare of a frightened rabbit. After a second or two, he shuddered and replied in a whisper, "We are not allowed."

"What do you mean, not allowed? What is going on?"

"You are not one of us," he answered, dropping each word as if a knife was piercing his lips. With that, he walked away briskly.

Lucia was baffled for a moment, disbelieving the next, and finally almost choking with rage. She slammed the cup on the table and went down to the lowest deck, where the crew quarters were located. She asked the first person in uniform she ran into, "I want to see the captain." The man nodded, took her by the arm, and escorted her down a corridor to a large cabin that was obviously the ship's main office. Entering through the open door, Lucia found herself facing a seated, bearded man, dressed all in white: jacket, pants, and hat. The jacket had gold trim along the cuffs, gold buttons, and decorative epaulets; the man wore a peaked cap with gold trim. Astonished at first, the captain got up, made a courteous bow, and asked in a clipped, British-sounding tone, "How may I assist you, madam?"

Lucia was taken aback by the question, for she was not sure of what exactly she wanted. Finally, she pulled herself together and replied, "I've a complaint. Your staff is apparently forbidden to talk to me. What's the matter?"

The captain appeared confused. "Has anybody told you that he is prohibited from talking to you? Because this cruise line prides itself on the excellent service it provides to our honored guests."

"Well, one of your waiters just said that I wasn't one of them. What does that mean?"

"Ah, that!" retorted the captain airily. "I'm sorry, most of our crew members are from various parts of Eastern Europe, Hungary, Serbia, Romania. Their English is limited, so they are instructed not to speak to our guests any more than necessary, to avoid misunderstandings. If you need to talk to anybody, talk to me, or the purser, or any of the other officers onboard. Any one of us will be able to give you satisfaction, I assure you." There was an insincere tone in the captain's explanation that left Lucia unsatisfied, but there was not much more she could do. She thanked the captain and retreated to her cabin.

She was still tense. She changed into her swimming suit and went upstairs to take a dip in the hot tub, an oval enclosure with walls covered by lapis lazuli and aqua tiles. She entered the tub at one end of the oval and crouched, neck deep, in the steaming waters, sensing how her body and mind relaxed amidst the vapors. She felt drowsy and was about to fall asleep when the noise of a splash at the other end of the oval startled her back to consciousness. Shaking herself alert, she noticed that others had entered the tub: a large woman in her thirties and a boy, no more than six or seven. The boy was pounding on the hot water, releasing cascades of steaming liquid all around; some droplets reached Lucia, startling her.

"Say, madam, could you please ask your child to stop splashing around?" she asked in a firm, somewhat annoyed voice. The woman looked in her direction and said nothing. The child spun his head and looked around the tub, peeking past Lucia, giving no sign of recognition.

Lucia bolted out of the tub and ran back to her cabin, shivering but not stopping to dry herself. She locked the door and plunged into her bed, still shaking.

She recovered after a while and felt hungry. She was not ready to face the dining room, so she ordered a meal from room service and asked for a glass of scotch, neat. The liquor would be charged to her account as a supplement, but she needed the splurge: she must have something to calm her nerves.

A somber waiter delivered her food and served it silently on her desk. She said nothing to him and did not give him a tip.

It got late but Lucia could not summon sleep. She paced restlessly back and forth in her cabin and at last made a decision. She put on her party dress and went up to the ballroom. It was Viennese night, said the daily newsletter. She had not waltzed for twenty years, but she was in a dangerous mood. She would finally have a good time, and if not, she would leave the ship in Athens and give up on this awful cruise.

As she entered the ballroom, the party was in full swing. A dozen couples were twirling around to the strains of "Voices of Spring." As she stopped to take in the sights, a wigged young waiter in costume approached her deftly, handed her a champagne flute and, taking her arm, escorted her to an empty table at the edge of the dance floor where she had a full view of the action.

At first, she watched the gyrations and admired the finery that some of the female passengers were sporting—everyone seemed to be attired differently, from Victorian gowns of light materials to strapless dresses and tee shirt outfits. A few unattached men came and went, all seemingly in search of something. A couple of them hovered in the vicinity of her table, but after making brief eye contact with Lucia, walked on.

Lucia slowly sank into despair. She did not know why she had come, what she was expecting to find in this ocean of humanity. She had never felt so lonely and started to cry silently.

A hand rested softly on her arm. She raised her head and there was a man, bent solicitously over her heaving shoulders. *"Cara signora, perchè piange così?"*

"I'm sorry, my Italian is quite rusty," replied Lucia, quickly wiping her tears.

"I apologize," said the man, in heavily accented English. "I was wondering, why are you crying? It's a beautiful night, and that spring-awakening music lifts the spirits. You should be out there dancing, not sitting in a corner like a widow in mourning."

"I'm a recent widow," replied Lucia. "I'm alone in the world, and nobody cares about me. I can't even get people to answer when I talk to them." She hiccupped and got ready to begin crying again.

"Come, dance with me. It'll make you feel better."

Lucia wanted to tell the stranger to go away, but he was the first person who had shown her kindness, and it would have been ungrateful to dismiss him. "All right, but I'm not a good dancer. Watch your feet."

The man shrugged dismissively and started to assist Lucia to get up. Just then, the orchestra finished playing "Voices of Spring" and paused to get ready for the next selection. The man sat next to Lucia.

As they waited, Lucia took a closer look at her rescuer. He was not young; probably as old as she, thinning gray hair and a face with deep wrinkles on the forehead and the edges of the mouth. He was solidly built and accompanied his speech with strong gestures. A man of action, no doubt. He did not look at all like her lamented husband but had a similar air, and the vague resemblance hurt her like a fresh stab to her heart.

To clear her mind from these morbid thoughts, she looked up (he was taller than she by more than a head) and asked, "I'm Lucia. What's your name?"

"My name is Marcello. I'm a painter from Lucca, in Toscana. That's in Italy, you know?"

"I do. Are you on vacation?"

"No, I'm working here on this ship. I was hired to restore some murals in the main dining room. It seems that steam from the buffet table damaged the paintings and I'm tasked with retouching and repainting, as needed."

Lucia sighed. "I'm taking my first cruise. My husband died recently and I'm trying to find a way to live by myself, alone." She did not mean to open up like this to a complete stranger but felt relief by sharing her predicament.

"I'm sorry for your loss," replied Marcello. "How are you liking the cruise so far?"

Lucia wanted to utter some bland nonsense, but again felt compelled to tell the truth. "Not well. People ignore me, and the staff is under orders not to answer my questions. Even tonight, nobody has sought to speak to me. You are the first…"

"Ah. I understand now. Perhaps you were not yet ready."

"What do you mean?"

"What's the last thing you remember doing before you came on board?"

"I was in the departure lounge, waiting to board the cruise… It got very stuffy; they had the heat set high and it was not that cold outside, so I felt a little faint…"

"Ah, Lucia. I have some bad news."

"What?"

"You must have had a heart attack or something. All this time you have probably been teetering between life and death. You were allowed on this ship because it was clear that you were not going to make it, but you couldn't be fully treated as a passenger as long as you were alive... You must have died just minutes ago, since I was able to approach and talk to you without crossing any barriers."

"Am I... am I dead?"

"I'm afraid so. This ship only comes ashore to collect dead passengers." He seized her hand and got her up on her feet. "Your hands are very cold. Let me warm them up." He took her right hand in his and planted a loving kiss on it.

"But yours are freezing also!"

He spoke softly in her ear, "Of course. Now, will you stroll with me around this modern version of *The Flying Dutchman?*"

"Yes, please," she whispered.

They vanished into the night, as the orchestra started playing the haunting notes of Saint-Saëns "Danse Macabre" for the remaining couples in the ballroom.

THE VILLAGE

That was the first I ever heard of shadowed Innsmouth. Any reference to a town not shown on common map or listed in recent guidebooks would have interested me, and the agent's odd manner of allusion roused something like real curiosity. A town able to inspire such dislike in it its neighbors, I thought, must be at least rather unusual, and worthy of a tourist's attention.
- H. P. Lovecraft, "The Shadow Over Innsmouth"

Near the end of 1928, I decided to take a short vacation to a remote island off the coast of Africa. After three days of touring all over the island and seeing every point of interest, I set my aim toward a small village I could see atop a tall hill across the bay.

The nasty remarks by the people at the resort in response to my inquiries both surprised and egged me on. I was irritated by the way the townsfolk made fun of a tourist for asking about the village. "That pimple on the butt of the world?" "Why are you asking about it?" "It's trash, just a bunch of lowlifes rutting in hovels like swine." "You shouldn't waste your time going to that dump, really."

A shopkeeper took me aside and whispered in my ear, "There are stories of people who went there and haven't been seen again."

Despite the taunting, as I looked from the balcony of my hotel room the village did not seem trashy at all—a cluster of whitewashed cottages with red tile roofs at the foot of a high hill, shimmering in the morning sunshine. The view of the bay from the top of that hill should be nice and would be worth a visit, as I had already taken enough pictures of every other corner of the island and still had two days left of my vacation. So, I decided to ignore the negative comments and go investigate.

Getting to Los Juanes—that was the name of the village—was not easy. There was apparently no bus service, so I decided to make it a day-long excursion and got on my rented bicycle, hoping to burn off some of the extra weight I had put on from too many cocktails. A dirt road spurted from the outskirts of town and seemed to meander aimlessly for miles before turning eastward and beginning to climb. After two hours of pedaling, I was exhausted, but I pressed on until I reached the foot of the hill that I had seen from across the bay. The hill was too steep for me to climb on the bicycle, so I leaned it against a centenary oak and proceeded on foot.

I was near the summit when two men emerged from the woods. They were dressed in outdoor clothes and wore plaid caps that covered their ears. Each carried what appeared to be an antique hunting rifle. Close to them circled three menacing-looking hounds.

I was startled by the sudden appearance of the men but greeted them. "Good morning, gentlemen. Nice day, isn't it?"

"Hello," responded one of the men, curtly. "What brings you to these parts?"

"Oh, nothing much. I came to see the view of the bay from this hill and check out the town."

The man grimaced. "It may not be a good idea for you to go into Los Juanes."

"Why not?"

"We've come from town chasing a fox that was seen acting suspiciously and may be rabid. She's probably somewhere around here, but may have doubled back and could be lurking anywhere."

"Will it be safe for me to go to the top of the hill and snap a few pictures?"

The second man replied with the same brusqueness. "You are safe if you stay around only a few minutes, but after that you should leave."

"All right." I agreed, disappointed. I continued climbing the steep path, and after a few minutes, I reached a ledge where I could see the bay and the town from which I had come.

The view was outstanding. It was the afternoon of a partly cloudy day, and the cottages and mansions were suffused in a golden light that rendered every feature a bit magical. Even my hotel, a utilitarian box of no architectural interest, resembled a wedding cake festooned with bright rectangles as the light bounced off closed windows. I took several pictures and would have gone for more but I realized it was getting late and it would not have been wise to linger.

As I turned around to leave, I glanced back and, out of the corner of my eye, caught a glimpse of a figure that was too large to be a fox. It was erect and moved quickly, so I lost sight of it almost at once, but not before I got a distinct impression that it was human—yet not quite so. I became somewhat alarmed and accelerated my downhill progress.

I returned to the spot where I had left my bicycle and began making a quick return to town. As daylight faded, I accelerated my downhill pedaling, until suddenly, I struck a deep pothole on the road and was thrown over the bicycle, which careened and collided with the trunk of a tree. I sustained several painful bruises, but the bicycle fared much worse: the front wheel was cracked and had collapsed.

After a bit of cursing, I stopped to consider my situation. Walking back to my hotel would be treacherous since, once it got dark, I would not be able to see the ground ahead of me and could trip on a hole or a stone and take another nasty fall. After pondering options for a while, I decided to brave the fox and give Los Juanes a try. I would look there for an inn or some other place to spend the night.

The village was a disappointment. The town's only street was unpaved; with every step I took, clouds of dust were released into the air. Most houses were one-floor stucco cottages in various stages of disrepair; some were missing roof tiles, others exhibited large wall cracks, and the white paint covering the plaster was peeling off many. I searched in vain for a tavern where I could make inquiries and perhaps grab some food; hotels, inns, or other public accommodations were conspicuously absent. This was a town that made no provisions for visitors.

I had made a circuit around Los Juanes and was approaching a road that led away, towards the mountains farther to the east, when I noticed what appeared to be a small church tucked away at the end of an alley, hiding as if ashamed of the poverty of its parishioners. Unlike the rest of the town, the white stucco building was in reasonable shape—all its Spanish clay tiles were firmly planted on the roof, no cracks or stains in evidence. There was no cross, but a small tower on top of the structure held an iron bell that would presumably ring to call the faithful to prayer.

I approached the building reluctantly, for I am not a religious person, but this seemed like the only possible way for me to get help. The door, made of dark wood, was covered with carvings whose nature I could not discern. I pressed on the door, and it creaked as it yielded. Without hesitation, I pushed it open all the way and walked in.

It was, and yet was not, a church. There was an empty altar, devoid of decorations, at the end of a long, narrow nave. Stained glass windows on opposite walls let in the failing afternoon light, imprinting it with a multitude of colors; there were no candles or artificial lights adding illumination to the scene. Pews had been removed and replaced by fourteen armchairs set in a circle around a large wooden table. No images of saints, pictures \, or other decorations were set on the walls or on the tiled floors.

As I was examining the strange arrangement, a side door opened behind the altar and from it emerged a very old man wearing an ankle-length cassock. He advanced haltingly as if fighting pain; in his right hand he carried a lit taper resting in a bronze holder. The flame from the taper wavered, as the man's grip seemed unsteady.

The man stopped a few steps from me and waved me to approach the table in the center of the room. He motioned for me to sit on one of the armchairs and deposited himself gingerly on another, two seats away. "What can I do for you, son?" he inquired in a grating voice that resembled the rasping of branches in the autumn wind.

"Father, I found myself in this village by accident and need a place to spend the night before returning to my hotel across the bay. Can you help me find shelter?"

The old man was silent for a long moment. "That's a problem," he started. "This is a poor village that seldom sees visitors. We have no public accommodations, and the people here do not take well to strangers."

"What can I do, then? Sleep on the ground outdoors?"

The man must have noticed the rising panic in my voice. He replied, "No, that would not be advisable...." He then added, with obvious reluctance, "I suppose you could stay here until tomorrow... I could set up a cot in the sacristy..."

"Oh, thank you, thank you. I promise I'll be gone by dawn."

"You can stay, on one condition."

"Anything."

"You must remain in the sacristy all night and not come to this room, no matter what you hear."

I blanched at the strange request and the stern manner of its delivery but nodded in agreement.

The man rose with an effort from the armchair. "Have you eaten?"

"No. I couldn't find any restaurant or tavern."

"Follow me. I may have some food in the sacristy."

We went through the door behind the altar into a dark room, much of which was occupied by a cabinet with many drawers, presumably containing vestments and other liturgical objects. There were two long tapers lit on a candelabrum on top of the cabinet, casting random shadows on the room as they flickered in a slight breeze coming from somewhere up high. The rest of the room held a lavatory, a table holding a large missal, and a bell over the door that would alert the congregation of the advent of the clergy. A small window near the ceiling let in the light of the early stars.

The man opened a closet and pulled out a folding cot, which, after opening, occupied almost all the empty space in the room. "Here," he pronounced. "I'll bring you sheets and a blanket in a minute. In the meantime, have this." He opened the top drawer of the cabinet and took out a heel of stale bread, an ancient-looking chunk of salami redolent of coriander, and a flask of red wine.

I was reluctant at first to partake of the dubious goods but, all of a sudden, I felt an acute flash of hunger and set aside my qualms. As I began devouring the food, the old man went out by another door and returned after a while with a cushion to serve as a pillow, two sheets, and a blanket. "Help yourself," he instructed. "Good night." Without giving me time to express my thanks for his hospitality, he turned around and left the same way he had come.

The food was barely edible, the wine tasted sour, and, as I lay on the cot, its thin mattress provided no support for my aching back. No matter. Suddenly, I was dead tired, and as night fell, I slipped into a deep slumber.

* * *

Much later, I woke up with a start. The tapers in the candelabrum were burning low, and the sacristy seemed much darker than when I fell asleep, but nothing seemed out of the ordinary. Then I heard it: the bell over the door was tinkling loudly, as if an invisible hand was beckoning the faithful to a ceremony.

I approached the rebellious bell with trepidation, my heart drumming a fast tattoo inside my chest. As I reached for it, the sound ceased. Deep silence returned and I took a deep breath, relieved. My pocket watch read three thirty a.m., so I turned back towards the cot to resume my rest.

No sooner had I lay down than indistinct noises began filtering through the closed door, coming from the nave. At first, I heard the shuffling of feet, then the scraping of furniture as it moved over the floor tiles. Finally, a murmur like voices, began rising—initially at random, and then in unison as if reciting some prayer. Then there was the sound of the old man, rising sharply above the rest: "Let's come to order! I have grave news to share!" The hubbub ceased at once, and the voice of the old man continued for a bit, now too low to be heard in the sacristy.

Whatever the man said had a deep impact on the audience, for the moment he was finished there was a chorus of shouts, screeches, and what sounded like animal wails. "Silence!" bellowed the old man. "He is asleep next door and may hear us!!"

Instead of quieting down, the nave erupted in a cacophony of angry human and non-human screams. One voice then rose above the rest in a raw baritone that I recognized as belonging to one of the men I had met on the hill. "We can't let him get out! He has seen a J'ork!"

I had heard enough. I ran to the back door from which the man had come and gone earlier. It was locked. The room's window appeared too narrow and too far up the wall to provide an escape route.

As escape was impossible, I met the danger head-on. I grasped the only available weapon, the lit candelabrum, and ran into the nave. I was confronted by a mob scene: a crowd had gathered around the round table, where fourteen figures sat in various states of agitation. Two of them were the hunters I had encountered in the afternoon.

Half of those present seemed more or less human, but the rest were strange creatures with low skulls and prominent brow ridges above their eyes. They were hairy, stocky, and dressed in rags that barely covered their privates. The central parts of their faces protruded forward and were dominated by very big, wide noses. They were as ugly as anything I had seen outside a zoo.

I tried to get past them, moving purposefully towards the front door, but I was seized at once by a couple of the quasi-apes and forced back to the center of the room. I soon realized that any efforts at resistance would be unsuccessful.

I was shoved toward the round table. The old man that I had taken for a priest got up, made room for me to be seated, and stood behind me, holding me in position by pressing down on my shoulders. Despite his age and apparent infirmity, his grip was strong.

He addressed me, but his words were meant for the entire congregation. "Your coming to the Los Juanes area has been unfortunate. We keep patrols on the town's perimeter and the first hill to keep strangers out. The business we conduct with the rest of the island takes place during the day, in the center of town, and we try to minimize outside contact by sending carts to other villages to trade and buy necessities. We do our best to be unwelcoming, and for the most part, succeed in keeping visitors away. Somehow you managed to elude our guards and saw one of our friends. I thought that by confining you to the back room we would be able to keep you until it was safe to release you, but it was not to be." He paused, as if reluctant to proceed.

"Now you have met what I would call some unusual members of our community. What you have seen cannot be unseen. The question is what to do with you now to protect their privacy."

At these words, there were shouts of "Kill him!" "He has to die!" "Like we did to the Italians," and other threats and grunts. The old man pounded on the table and demanded: "Silence! We are not animals. We'll give due consideration to the situation and all the risks involved, and then decide what course of action is the best!"

He turned to me again, "I'm afraid that we will need to put you under guard for the time being. You will go back to the room where you slept."

* * *

I lost track of time and could not remember exactly how long I had been confined in the room. In a drawer in the cabinet was a thin stack of prayer books, and I started writing notes in the margins with a stubby pencil I found.

Judging by the number of books I filled, at least a couple of weeks went by; my unkempt beard was also an indicator of the duration of my ordeal. If the townspeople in the resort where I stayed could have seen my condition, their smirks would have turned to derisive laughs.

I was visited daily by someone from the village who came to bring me food, clean the bathroom, and sweep the floor. They were always dour women who resisted my attempts to draw them into conversation. I had not seen the old man again, nor any of the male inhabitants of Los Juanes. They kept me in complete ignorance of what was going on in this village or what they intended to do with me, but the reference to "the Italians" was unnerving.

A few days after the start of my confinement, a fresh face showed up with my dismal dinner. It was a middle-aged woman that appeared distraught as she paced around the room. "You look sad," I commented, expecting silence in return.

"My husband died yesterday." She broke down into tears.

I walked up to her and circled my arm around her shoulders. "I'm sorry to hear that," I instinctively responded. Her body heaved under my touch. Then, unexpectedly, she went on. "Those brutes killed him."

I held my breath. "Which brutes?" I asked, as softly as I could.

"The J'ork," she replied. "I hate 'em!"

That was the opening I needed. "Who are they?"

Between crying fits, she told an astonishing story.

"The first settlers of the village, over two centuries ago, were a knot of immigrants from the mainland led by two cousins, Juan Francisco Meléndez and Juan José de Armas, who named the settlement 'Los Juanes' after themselves. A few weeks after the initial efforts to establish a town, one of the colonists came upon a young child roaming the hill. It was a creature that looked more like a hairy ape than a human. The captive fought fiercely but was subdued, brought to the village, and placed in a cage. All efforts to communicate with him were answered with snarls and guttural cries.

"That night, as the colonists sat around the fire near their half-finished huts, four adult creatures appeared from the darkness. They were armed with rudimentary clubs and advanced toward the villagers, making threatening gestures and swinging their weapons. Juan Meléndez got up and calmly approached them, waving his arm in salutation.

"The leader of the creatures raised a club and aimed for his head. Everything seemed lost, but Meléndez started a pantomime in which he imitated a crying child, pointed to the visitors, and inquired, in words and gestures, 'Is he one of yours?'

"The creature lowered his club and nodded. Meléndez asked his cousin in a low voice, 'Fetch the little monster and bring him here.' A few moments later, Juan de Armas returned, holding the child. No sooner did he and the visitors see each other, than they rushed to meet and one of the creatures seized him and held him close in its arms.

"Meléndez turned to the group's leader and pointing to the meat roasting on a spit on the fire, made signs of hunger and invited the visitors to join them in supper. All partook of the food, and Meléndez passed around a leather bota bag full of red wine. At first, the visitors looked at the wineskin suspiciously, but their leader put it to his mouth, took a swig, and opened his eyes wide with surprise and pleasure. He immediately handed it to one of his companions.

"The colonists and the strange visitors had a convivial meal together and Meléndez started conducting a sign language conversation with them. An hour later, when the visitors had become tipsy and sated, they returned to the woods. Colonists and creatures motioned goodbye to each other amicably.

"When they were gone, Meléndez turned to his companions. 'I think we have made an amazing discovery. Whatever we do, let's keep the existence of these creatures to ourselves. I'll write to my uncle, the priest, to see if he knows anything about them and can recommend what we should do. He is a wise and learned man.'

"While letters were exchanged back and forth with the Continent, the colonists got to see the creatures many times. They seemed to understand the rudiments of human language but were unable to speak. They referred to themselves as the J'ork and lived in caves in the hills around Los Juanes. They used wood and made sharpened stone tools, knew fire, and survived by hunting small animals, digging roots, and eating berries. Despite their bestial appearance, they appeared somewhat intelligent.

"After a very long wait, Meléndez heard back from his uncle. 'All I have been able to find out is rumor, legend, and conjecture. Old wives' tales claim that once men shared the earth with other, more primitive beings that were similar to them but less advanced. Over time, men overcame and extinguished those beings. Their existence is not mentioned in the Holy Books or any of the histories of the various peoples of the earth. So, I must conclude that the tales are just myths. On the other hand, it is possible that the creatures once existed, and a handful have survived on your isolated island. I caution you to keep your finding secret until you are ready to reveal it to the world.'

"Meléndez followed his uncle's admonition. When Los Juanes was finished and everyone moved in, they purposefully isolated themselves from the rest of the island to prevent discovery of their odd neighbors. A few months later, Meléndez died of a fever and de Armas became head of the colony. He retained the veil of secrecy instituted by his cousin, and little by little the two groups became closer to each other. Early the following year, a female J'ork gave birth to a child who partook of the traits of both her parents: she was taller and thinner than her mother and had humanlike features, marred by a pronounced brow and a wide nose. As the two races started interbreeding, thoughts of revealing the existence of the J'ork were abandoned.

"Things stayed peaceful until Father Manich arrived," continued the woman. "He had been sent from the Continent to establish new parishes on the island. But he is a rude and ill-tempered man, and other towns came to reject him and sought his recall. Instead of returning home, however, he came to Los Juanes and convinced the population here that there was a need for a proper religious center. Some wanted to lynch him, but a majority agreed to build him a church instead. When I was born, the church was already up and in use.

"Father Manich learned early of the existence of the J'ork and became convinced that it was his moral duty to evangelize them. His efforts always met indifference or actual resistance. Finally, he gave up trying to convert the savages and turned the church that had been built into a social center where members of both races could gather. That's where we are today."

"Why do you still hide the J'ork from the rest of the world?" I asked, incredulously.

"We are largely related to them by now. Also, the J'ork are at least equal in numbers to us humans, and we fear there could be a bloody encounter if the J'ork learned we were going to betray them. The J'ork can be quite violent. Recently, there have been brawls over food between J'ork and humans. My husband was killed in one of those."

I took advantage of my new familiarity with the woman to make a request. "I am very thankful for the long story you have told me. Now, could you do me another big favor?"

Her eyes narrowed. "What?"

"Could you get me a table? I spend all day sitting on that chair but have no place to rest my arms or put a plate of food when it's brought to me."

"I'll see what I can do."

* * *

Every night, after the church quieted down, I climbed on the table and set to work on the plaster around the window frame using an iron crucifix whose head I had laboriously sharpened as my tool. I constantly feared that my efforts would be discovered, or that my captors would finally decide to do away with me, or that the enlarged opening of the window would still be too narrow to allow me to get through, or that I would break something when I jumped down to the courtyard, or that I would be captured and put to death. I was besieged by an army of worries.

Yet I was undeterred and continued to work away at the plaster, which was crumbly and broke off easily. And one night, I finished removing a thumb's width of frame from all around the window. I carefully took the window down, slats and hinges and all, and set it on the table.

I left the prayer books with my story in the cabinet where I found them. If I made it out and was able to escape, I would be able to tell the story on my own and bring justice to this godforsaken town. If I failed, someone might someday discover the narrative of my confinement and remember me with pity.

* * *

I barely squeezed through the window's hole, got lost as I went through Los Juanes in the dark, and stumbled and fell a couple of times as I fled madly away. I almost cleared the village, but as I reached its outskirts I was confronted by a small, non-human figure: a young J'ork, barely in his teens.

I never knew what the youth was doing out in the middle of the night; presumably, it was his turn to patrol the village to spot strangers. Whatever his mission, he came at me swinging a club and screaming in a shrill voice in an attempt to raise the alarm.

I panicked. I jumped at him to throttle his cries and we fought. He was strong for his age, but I was driven by desperation, so I overpowered him and to my eternal shame, lost my self-control. The fear and resentment that had accumulated during my imprisonment exploded in a whirlwind of rage; I wrestled the club from his hands and started beating him over the head, on his arms and chest, wherever

I could land a blow.

It was over in a minute. After the first couple of blows he stopped resisting and lay on the ground, unable to parry my attacks. But I did not let up. I kept beating his body to a bloody pulp, until I stopped, exhausted, and gazed at the immobile figure beneath me. I had killed him.

I then continued running until I was overcome by exhaustion. In the early morning, I was picked up not far from the resort by an oxen-driven cart laden with coal. I was barely conscious, battered and bleeding, so the cart driver took me to a dispensary where nuns cared for my wounds and let me rest for a couple of days before allowing the police constable to interrogate me.

As I lay waiting for the officer's visit, I was assaulted by doubt. Should I reveal what I had seen and experienced? Vindication would give me pleasure, but the boy's slaying would probably be revealed, and I would have to face justice for my actions.

When the officer arrived, I said that I had fallen in the hills, injured my head, and had been wandering aimlessly for many days, suffering from amnesia. I could tell he did not believe my story, but no crime had been exposed and I was left alone.

I tried to rationalize my silence on grounds other than trying to hide my culpability. The people of Los Juanes and the J'ork had lived in harmony for over a couple of centuries. Did I have the right to disturb their peace? Who knows what the "civilized" world would do to these lost ancestors of the human race? Put them in cages and display them in zoos? Turn them over to the scientists for their experiments? Men are cruel to anyone who is weaker or different.

I also told myself that I owed no debt of gratitude to the inhabitants of Los Juanes, human or J'ork, and the death of the youth was their own fault. I wanted to leave the island quietly and avoid further entanglements that might land me in prison or hold me there for a long time.

I returned home, but the memory of Los Juanes has traveled back with me. I was bedeviled by daytime fears and assaulted by nightmares. I suffered until one day, I came to understand that all I felt was fear of retribution, not remorse. The villagers of Los Juanes and the J'ork were miserable creatures that deserved punishment. The slaying of one of their number was only scant retribution for the ills they had visited on me. I relived in my mind the bone-crushing blows I had inflicted on the young savage and the memory brought me only an odd satisfaction.

The discovery of the J'ork has yet to occur. I attribute this to the remoteness of the island and the enforced isolation of the village on the hill. Yet, their existence coming to light is inevitable, and if civilization finds the J'ork while I am alive, my misgivings may come to life. For that reason, it will be fine by me if the secrets of Los Juanes remain shrouded in mystery for a little bit longer.

In the meantime, I will continue to struggle with the pangs of my conscience. I am certainly not a better person than when I went on this fateful vacation; indeed, I am more callous and less respectful of human life than I was then. I made a great discovery but derived no benefit from it and will have to live with its consequences the rest of my days.

ROSALBA

O Lola c'hai di latti la cammisa/
si bianca e russa comu la cirasa,
quannu t'affacci fai la vucca a risa,/
biatu pì lu primu cu ti vasa!
Ntra la puorta tua lu sangu è spasu,/
ma nun me mpuorta si ce muoru accisu...
e si ce muoru e vaju 'n paradisu/
si nun ce truovo a ttia, mancu ce trasu.

O Lola, your dress is white as milk,/
you are white and red like a cherry,
your lips smile when you look through the window,/
blessed is he who gives you the first kiss!
Your threshold is sprinkled with blood,/
and I don't care if I'm killed there.
And if I die and go to Paradise,/
if I don't find you there, I will not even enter.
- Pietro Mascagni, *Cavalleria Rusticana,* Scene 1

I leave home at daybreak. I get on the dirt road by the hut and go on a steady uphill walk toward the ruined town. I take no notice of the scurrying little beasts that seek to end a night of foraging without becoming prey to an owl or a falcon. As I advance to higher ground, the dark barren hillocks the locals call *calanchi* come into view. Their stark beauty is all too familiar, and I ignore them.

At the town's gate, which is boarded to keep intruders away, I run—as I often do—into the shepherd boy that leads his goats and the mule he calls Clarissa crosstown toward the pastures to the west. He cannot be older than nine and has the striking, mixed-race looks of the natives of Basilicata. He bends his head respectfully (perhaps fearfully) and mutters a greeting or a prayer I do not hear. I wave at him and move on.

I cross the overgrown streets of the ancient town, avoiding the debris that covers the ground, always going uphill. I pass structures fallen into ruin, decrepit palaces and churches still showing remnants of the shutters, railings, and frescoes that once graced them. At last, I arrive at the chosen meeting place. Rosalba awaits me, standing by a stone slab that serves as a bench at the entrance of the highest structure in the city, the long-abandoned Norman Tower. She is pale, but her features remain as beautiful as ever.

"You are late," she complains in a voice laden with recrimination.

"I am not," I reply flatly and sit next to her.

I try to hold her hand but, as always, Rosalba shies from my touch. "What do you have to say for yourself?" she asks with asperity.

"Nothing much" I reply. "I spend most of the time thinking about you, about us, about the life we used to have."

"Bah!" replies Rosalba dismissively. "Even in the best of times, our life was nothing to brag about. You worked the fields, I cared for our home, we went together to Sunday Mass and to the festival of Saint Vincenzo in October. One boring season after another, year after year."

"But there was always love."

"Perhaps at first. Then your jealousy destroyed all we had."

"There was a reason for jealousy. Can you deny that the town men made eyes at you, that you returned their glances and flirted with them?"

"Well, a woman always likes to be admired. It was not my fault to be pretty. But in my heart, I was always faithful to you."

"Always?"

"Always."

"How can you say that? You know it is not true. I caught you right here in the arms of Tulio, that filthy baker from Potenza."

"Tulio meant nothing to me. Only a passing fancy, though there was more than that on his part. He was handsome and virile and treated me with respect. Every day he would bake a wonderful loaf of Pane di Matera for us and bring it over to our hut, as a gift."

"And you sold yourself to him for a loaf of bread!" The fury that never goes away fills my mouth with bile.

"Not so. I felt I owed him a few kisses in exchange for his kindness. We came to this abandoned tower to be away from the town gossips. I never lay with him, never touched him, before you caught us…"

"I can't believe you still claim you were faithful to me! *Putana!*" I rise from the stone slab and wave a menacing fist at her.

Rosalba utters a thin laugh. "You can't hurt me anymore than you did."

"I did what I had to do," I groan.

"You found us together in this tower and murdered us both."

"I had been following you, and by the time I got here I was too angry to control my actions."

"You knifed Tulio twice on the chest and that was that for him. He was almost peaceful as he died in my arms. But what you did to me…"

"Please, stop!" I beg.

Rosalba goes on, implacable. "You butchered me and buried me while I was still not quite dead!" Her voice rises in a dark torrent.

"Please, stop!" I beg again, in vain.

"You dug a hole in the dirt and dumped me there. That mound marks the spot."

"I know…" I whimper.

"I lie there, in the cold earth, without a Christian burial, without a hearse, food for the wolves and the maggots, like a dead animal."

"I had to bury you. I feared I would be charged with murdering you if your body was discovered."

"At least you dragged Tulio's body away and dropped it on the main road, where he would be found. He rests in peace. But I…"

"I would love to remove you from the earth and give your remains a proper burial, if I only could…"

"You cannot, and I forbid it."

"But then, please, release me from these encounters!" I beg. "I cannot endure the torment."

"Yet you feel no remorse for your actions. You still think your murders were justified. You regret nothing!"

"It's too late for regrets," I cry.

Our bickering continues, in endless repetition, through the day and into the late afternoon. As the sun starts setting, Rosalba says with finality, "You are beyond redemption. So, I will never release you. I command you to return tomorrow. Don't be late."

Rosalba's figure becomes immaterial, translucent, almost invisible as it sinks to the earth beneath the little mound. I remain sitting on the stone slab, watching without seeing how my long-dead wife disappears for another day. A cloud drifts across the late afternoon sky and everything is suddenly engulfed in darkness. A gust of the wind that always blows on this hill elicits groans and creaks from the deserted houses below.

I have lingered too long in my daily dispute with Rosalba's ghost; the last strands of pink sunset light fade from the tops of the *calanchi*. I get up slowly and go inside the building. Finding my way by touching the walls, I ascend a long set of stone steps that takes me to the square roof of the tower. There I remain for a long time, watching as night creeps over the countryside. It had been painful for me to watch from this vantage point when the townspeople had to move away because the landslides and quakes made it unsafe for them to remain.

The view of the deserted town below, cast in shadows in

the fading twilight, envelopes me like a shroud of melancholy. What is left for me? All that I once loved was gone, taken away by my own hand. I should go away forever, as the townspeople did.

I climb onto the parapet that encircles the top of the tower and balance myself against the rising evening wind. Should I do it? Why not? What is there to linger on for?

As I crouch to gather momentum for the fatal plunge to the cobblestones below, I have a strange sense of familiarity, as if the muscles of my thighs are readying for a practiced exercise. I take a deep breath and leap.

Midway through the air, though, I remember—as I do every night at this moment—that the release I seek is forever being denied me. Like many previous jumps, this one cannot possibly kill me. The first one, years ago, already did.

OPAQUE

*The aura given out by a person or object is as much
a part of them as their flesh.*
- Lucian Freud

Even in the early days, before the city expanded deeply into the suburbs, the property was an anomaly. It was a large parcel of land, about a city block long and half a block wide, weed-covered and empty save for a clapboard house with white paint starting to peel away and a rusted tin roof that sat at the front of the lot, facing the highway. Everything about the house spoke of decline and old age—everything except a carefully drawn sign announcing in oversized red capitals: SPIRITUAL ADVISOR, followed below in slightly smaller capitals by PSYCHIC READINGS, and further below that, under a drawing of an open hand flanked with sun, moon, and stars, an even smaller entreaty to UNLOCK YOUR SOUL'S AWAKENING.

There was plenty of space to park in a graveled rectangle behind the house, but visitors appeared to be few, and the lot seemed empty most of the time. Nonetheless, those who regularly drove by could see the sign, upright and well-kept, standing guard before the house. The "spiritual advisor" remained in business through booms and busts, the dark green front door opening briefly from time to time to admit or discharge a client.

Gareth Flint—Garry to his business associates—was not in search of enlightenment. As a junior executive at the city's largest real estate developer, Garry assiduously searched for projects that would advance his career. It was during one of his scouting drives through the suburbs that, early one morning, he came upon the clapboard house with the strange sign in front. He stationed his car in the parking area and made his way to the house.

The door was closed. This was no surprise since most places of business would not open for a couple of hours. He knocked gently on the door.

After a while, shuffling steps approached and the door was opened partway. An old woman in a frayed pink night-gown stood before him. She was thin and mahogany in color and stood erect like an overgrown cinnamon stick. Her face was a mass of wrinkles, and the only parts that seemed alive were piercing black eyes that looked through Garry as if assessing each part of him. "Can I help you?" she asked in a thin, papery voice that seemed to come from somewhere else far away.

Garry was taken slightly aback but quickly composed himself. "I am sorry I am here at this early hour. I was driving by and noticed your sign, and was curious as to what services you provide. I can come back later…"

"Never mind," she cut him off. "I was already up. Please come in." She opened the door all the way and Garry stepped into another world.

The living room, if that is what the main room in the house was, was filled to overflowing with objects of all kinds and sizes, thrown together haphazardly. Elaborate urns held arrangements of paper flowers; dolls of all sizes dressed in American, European, and Japanese gowns sat on tables and chairs and even on the carpeted floors, and were surrounded by stuffed monkeys, tigers, raccoons, and other animals. There were also bird cages holding replicas of cockatoos, peacocks, woodpeckers—even a disturbing, life-like raven. Several cases full of fake jewelry, feathers, ker-chiefs, scarves, coins, glassware, swatches of fabric, and books in several languages added to the confusion. Only a large, sloped chaise lounge covered in a faded velvet fabric and an ancient wingback chair placed across from the sofa were free of clutter.

The old woman motioned Garry towards the chaise lounge, and as he sat there, she primly deposited herself on the chair. "What can I do for you, sir? What was there about the sign that caught your interest?"

Garry had to think quickly to come up with an excuse for his intrusion. His goal was to see if there was a way to acquire this property, but he realized that an old lady, probably living alone surrounded by junk, would not have a keen interest in a real estate transaction. So he assumed a bewildered air and asked, feigning confusion, "What kinds of psychic readings do you do? I have always been interested in those."

The old woman cleared her throat and launched into a well-rehearsed speech. "As you may know, there are many kinds of psychic readings. They are all intended to obtain information from or about a subject using the reader's unique perceptive abilities. Some of the more common types of readings include Tarot card readings, palm readings, astrological readings, and aura readings. Most of these are just worthless bunk intended to entertain or defraud the client. I only do aura readings, and occasionally read a subject's palm to confirm my findings."

"What are aura readings?"

"An aura is an energy field that surrounds a person or animal, though never an inanimate object. It is invisible, yet some practitioners have the ability to see the size, color and type of vibration of an aura."

"Where does that energy come from?"

"It is complicated. All forms of life simultaneously exist in two parallel dimensions, one the physical body and the other the non-physical realm of the mind known as the 'subtle body,' which is all energy, while the physical body is mass. The subtle body consists of energy channels connected by nodes of psychic energy called *chakras*. There are many chakras throughout the subtle body, but the most important are seven, all arranged along the spinal cord, from bottom to top.

"Each of those chakras releases psychic energy that feeds the aura. Since the mind plane interacts with the body plane, the amount and quality of the energy that is released to the aura varies with time and emotional and physical activity. The source and nature of these releases color the aura."

"So, when you read an aura, what do you do?"

"I hold the client's hands, close my eyes, empty my mind, and try to read into it the composition of his or her aura. Don't ask how I do it, but it happens."

"How do you interpret what you see?"

"From experience. After many years, I have learned what many of the shapes and colors of the auras mean. For example, if a person is in good health, his aura has a steady light green overtone, which is underlain by pulsating splashes of colors of various shapes and intensities. For a very old person, or one that is seriously ill, the green overtone is virtually gone. I once read the aura of a man who appeared in good health and discovered that the overtone of his aura was whitish yellow, and nearly gone. He died of pancreatic cancer barely two months after my reading."

"What other things can you tell from reading an aura?"

"If a person is experiencing a strong emotion, it will manifest itself in the aura by repeated bursts of vivid colors—one of the most common sights that I encounter, typically among my female clients, is a series of indigo bursts that tell me that the subject is experiencing overwhelming grief, as if she has lost someone dear and has not recovered. But the aura shows all kinds and gradations of feelings and emotions, and even the natural disposition of a person's character."

"Can you predict the future by reading a person's aura?"

"Only in the limited sense that physical disorders that may lead to disease can show in an aura. Otherwise, I can help you better know who you are but am not able to predict whether you will win the lottery or become a movie star. Sorry."

"Fascinating," noted Garry, trying to keep a straight face at the nonsense. His effort was not totally successful, as his lower lip protruded slightly in a pout.

"I see you are not convinced. Would you like a sample reading?"

"How much will it be?" asked Garry, a little alarmed.

"Nothing. I will just do a superficial reading, to show you how it is done."

"Well, okay."

"It will only be a few minutes. Give me your hands." The old woman reached from her chair and placed her thin hands above Garry's fleshy ones.

"Do I have to do anything?"

"Just relax." The woman closed her eyes and remained silent for a few minutes. Then she let Garry's hands go and shuddered. There was a frown on her face.

"What is the matter? Am I sick or something?"

"No, your aura is strong, but I notice some white streaks along with the green that overlies it."

"What does that mean?"

"Your health is okay now, but you are showing the initial signs of what could become heart trouble. You should exercise and watch what you eat. And drink only in moderation."

Garry, who was a few pounds overweight, smiled inwardly. *I bet she says the same thing to all her clients*, he thought. "What else did you see?"

"There is a thick orange line mixed with some violet bursts. You are ambitious and have placed your career goals ahead of any personal attachments." Garry, who was wearing an expensive-looking suit, concluded that this was again cheap psychology—he had arrived early in the morning, driving a late model black sedan, so anyone could draw those conclusions.

"I also saw a series of red spots on the upper portion of your aura. Have you had any chest or arm injuries lately?"

That question gave Garry some pause since he had sustained a torn ligament on his right shoulder while playing squash, and the injury had not totally healed so the shoulder hurt every time he raised his arm. But, again, that was either a lucky hit or something that most people were bound to acknowledge as a recent occurrence. Or perhaps she was a very good observer.

"I hurt my shoulder a couple of weeks ago, but the pain is almost gone." The lady frowned again and said nothing.

"What else did you see?" Garry asked, curious despite himself.

The old woman demurred. "I did not look long enough or deep enough to come up with more detailed findings. Come back for a formal reading and I will spend more time examining your aura, which I found quite interesting."

Garry was not going to fall for that. "I will," he promised insincerely. "But in the meantime, may I ask you a question?"

"Sure," said the woman.

"How long have you owned this house?"

The old woman's eyes became unfocused as if she was trying to do a mental calculation. "Well, the land has belonged to my family since the 1860s, and I think my grandfather built the house somewhere in the early part of the century. I was born here myself around that time, and as an only child, I inherited the property about 1950 when my father died. So, it must be forty years or more."

"How did your family get the land in the first place?"

"My great-great-grandfather was a slave working on a farm located here. Near the end of the Civil War, Union troops under General Sheridan occupied this area and the landowner and his family fled south toward Richmond. Sheridan ordered the landowner's home and other farm buildings razed, and later had the estate deeded to the former slaves to prevent the former owners from reclaiming it. By that time, only my great-great-grandfather and his family, along with a few other slaves, remained on the property. Over the years, he and his children sold off portions of his holdings so that only what you see remains in my hands."

"And you are the sole owner of the property?"

"Yes. My husband died fifteen years ago and we had no children." She pointed to a large, framed photograph of a middle-aged black man hanging from the wall opposite the chaise lounge. "Julian was a very good man."

"Would you be interested in selling this property and perhaps moving to a nice home in town? I am in the real estate business and could get you a very nice sum for it."

"Why would I do anything like that? My remaining days are few and I have little use for money. Plus, I always lived here and would never go away. My husband, my parents, my grandparents, my sister Sarah, and many other relatives are buried right behind this house. All the things you see here were gathered by my ancestors and remind me of them every day. Would I ever want to walk away? No." While the lady never raised her voice, the last sentences were said slowly, laying emphasis on every word.

Garry knew there was no point in arguing with the old biddy or trying to persuade her. He extracted a business card from his pocket and handed it to the lady. "Here is my card. If you change your mind or have any questions, please give me a call. By the way, what is your name?"

"Eliza Perkins. I was named after my great-grand-mother."

"Thank you for your hospitality, Mrs. Perkins. I hope to see you soon."

"Have a good day, sir."

* * *

Garry Flint did not give up easily on a potentially profitable transaction. Seeing that old Mrs. Perkins would not voluntarily let go of her property, he set out to find other means of getting it. The first step in every transaction of this type was research: he needed to find out the chain of title to the land in question, and if possible, trace it back to the pre-Civil War days, when white farmers owned it. A visit to the courthouse and the office of the recorder of deeds was both illuminating and frustrating. The oldest recorded title to the property was dated October 1864. It stated how, as ordered by General Philip Henry Sheridan, Commander of the Army of the Potomac, the estate formerly known as "The Johnson Preserve" was divided into ten equal parcels to be deeded to former slave workers on the property, who had remained there when "the treasonous title holder" fled to join the forces of the Confederacy. One Zebadiah Perkins was among the ten new owners.

Subsequent records revealed that over the next thirty years, the ten parcels had been consolidated into four, one of them held by a Burwell Perkins. In 1913, Burwell Perkins sold three smaller parcels of land to various people. No other title transfers were noted on what remained of Mr. Perkins's property.

From this information, Garry deduced that the original estate was fairly large, and today there were a minimum of seven parties, plus Mrs. Perkins, who owned pieces of it. Further discussions with the clerk of the circuit court revealed that the original courthouse, and the property records it contained, had been burned to the ground during General Sheridan's campaign, so it was not possible to identify the owner of the Johnson Preserve before it was seized by the Army of the Potomac.

Garry's curiosity and greed were vastly stimulated by the information he had gathered. With the help of a title search expert, he was able to reconstruct the boundaries of the Johnson Preserve and identify all current owners of portions of the estate. There were eleven parcels of various sizes, the one currently occupied by Mrs. Perkins being the second largest. The remaining parcels included six modest homes, a Baptist church, a restaurant, and two small stores. If the original Johnson Preserve could be reconstructed and brought under a single owner, it would be worth millions.

That night he placed a call to a lawyer on retainer to his real estate company who was also his squash partner, Edmund Knapp, Esq., known to his intimates as "Fast Eddie" for less than wholesome reasons. Garry posed the following question to him. "Eddie, if a man had real property in

Virginia that was seized by the Yankees during the Civil War, and that property was given out to a bunch of slaves, could the man or his descendants sue to get the property back as an illegal transfer?"

There was a short pause and Fast Eddie retorted, "He could always sue. Whether he would win would be something else."

"Come on, Eddie, I need to know if one of my clients has any chance of recovering what was rightfully his and was seized during the War Between the States. What do you know?"

"I recall that during the Civil War, there was legislation that allowed the government to seize properties belonging to disloyal persons, but I do not remember the details. Let me look into it and I will get back to you. Is there a client number for this to which I can charge my time?"

"Not yet, Eddie, but perhaps soon."

Two days later, Eddie called Garry. "I have good news and bad news. The story is complex but basically goes as follows. In 1863, Congress passed a law allowing the Department of Treasury or its agents to collect property in the insurrectionary territory whose owners had abandoned it in aid of the insurrection. The property was put under the temporary control of Union officials, ready to be returned to the owners after the war in the event that the owners' loyalty to the Union could be proved. The property was ordinarily put in the hands of tenants who were engaged to cultivate it. Later on, after the war was over, the Supreme Court held that Congress had intended to restore property not only to the loyal owners but all owners regardless of allegiance. But there was a catch to the right of restitution: under the original law, suits to seek such restitution had to be brought within two years of the suppression of the rebellion. So, your client may be out of luck."

"But there must be arguments that can be made in favor of someone in the position of my client. And you can come up with them, I am sure."

"Oh, yes. If there was litigation, I would argue that the

original seizure was illegal and that the government had no power to transfer title to the slaves. And I would argue that the owners were justified in not filing restitution claims within two years because they thought they could not prove loyalty. I am sure I can come up with many other arguments. But it is not clear to me right now which way a case would turn out."

"Fair enough. It is enough that he could sue without having his case dismissed out of hand. If the litigation is tangled up in court for months or years, we might be able to get settlements with the people currently occupying the properties. Do you think you could get that done?"

"Possibly."

"Then we may be in business. Let me work on my end and I will get back to you at some point in the future."

"Fine."

* * *

Garry thus developed a bold plan: if he could locate the former owners of Johnson Preserve and could prevail upon them to sue for restitution of the property, and if the legal challenge was successful, he could acquire the property and open it up for development in a massive project that would make him a very wealthy man.

An obsessive search consumed the next three years of Garry's life. Richmond was a big city and had experienced a lot of turmoil during the Civil War and its aftermath. Johnson was too common a name to be useful in itself. Garry spent countless weekends in Richmond, in libraries and local historical societies, combing through newspapers, memoirs, letters, and other records of the period hoping to find traces of the Johnsons who had sought refuge in the Richmond area when the Rebel cause disintegrated.

His life routine was changed by the search. He no longer exercised, took to heavy drinking and poor eating, and was worn out by the constant travel between Northern Virginia and Richmond. He came close several times to abandoning the quest, only to tell himself that he did not have anything better to do and to quit would mean returning to a mediocre life as a house peddler.

Then, when he least expected it, a nugget of gold washed in with the silt and sediment in the pan of his search. He was skimming an article on the life of Confederate General Bushrod Johnson when he came upon a reference to a cousin of the general, one Thaddeus Johnson, whom he sometimes visited when reporting to the Confederacy's military headquarters in Richmond. Thaddeus and his family were once rich landowners but had been forced out of their Northern Virginia property by the brutal Northern campaign later known as "The Burning."

He now had a name to go on. Further research into "Thaddeus Johnson" led to a federal townhouse in New Town, a historic section of Petersburg, where a gentleman of that name had settled in the 1870s. The townhouse was in disrepair and showed signs of neglect going back many years.

Garry knocked on the door and was greeted by an ill-kept old man who identified himself only as Bert. When asked if this was the Johnson residence, Bert croaked, "You mean my girlfriend, Sally?" whereupon he loudly summoned a slovenly middle-aged woman. She confirmed her name was Sally and proceeded to relate how her ancestor Thaddeus had decided he could no longer afford to live in Reconstruction Era Richmond, had moved with his family to the less expensive nearby city of Petersburg, and had built this townhouse. Several generations of Johnsons had dwelt there; she was the last surviving member of the family.

Garry prompted her gently as to what she knew of the family history and their former holdings in Northern Virginia. She acknowledged that she was ignorant of any of that but noted that her dad had kept a number of old papers in a trunk that was stored in the attic. Controlling his excitement as best as he could, Garry asked if it would be too inconvenient for her to show him those papers since he was doing historical research and might find some of the information they contained useful.

Sally asked Bert to go get the trunk and while he was fetching it, she warned Garry slyly, "You can look however much you want, but you will have to pay for anything you take." Garry nodded benignly.

The trunk contained much that was worthless and almost all the rest was water-damaged and illegible. One thing that was fairly legible, however, was a collection of documents relating to the Johnson Preserve, including a copy of the title, tax payment receipts, and other business records. Garry told Sally soberly, "I would like to look at these more closely. May I take them with me and return them within a day or two?" She said he would have to pay twenty dollars in order to take them, and twenty more if he wished to keep them. He readily agreed.

Garry was gone for several days and returned to Petersburg in the company of Fast Eddie. They had a long meeting with Sally and Bert, which ended up in a three-part agreement. First, Fast Eddie would bring a restitution action on Sally's behalf. Second, if he ultimately succeeded in the action, Sally would immediately convey title to all the Johnson Preserve estate to a corporation, wholly owned by Garry, and would be paid fifty thousand dollars per acre of the estate. Third, if during the pendency of the suit, a settlement was reached with any of the current occupiers of the estate, Sally would convey title to that portion of the estate to Garry's corporation, and still would be paid fifty thousand dollars per acre for that portion of the estate; title to any improvements upon the land would also pass to the corporation. The corporation would pay for all the costs of litigation, including Fast Eddie's fees.

Sally was illiterate in business and legal matters and only saw her chance to get fifty thousand dollars or more without having to do anything, so the contracts—which Eddie had thoughtfully provided—were signed that same day. Bert and a lady living in the townhouse next door were happy to sign as witnesses.

* * *

When the suit was brought in a Virginia state court, it caused a big stir among the population, particularly the ethnic families that lived on or near the Johnson Preserve. Many were irate that an attempt would be made to disenfranchise people who had lived and worked peacefully on the land for a century. Others feared that a domino effect would be unleashed, affecting other properties that had remained out of the hands of Confederate supporters since the Civil War. The Baptist Church succeeded in getting the American Civil Liberties Union to assume the defense of their case on a pro-bono basis. The two small stores and the restaurant pooled their resources to hire a local lawyer to represent them. The private property owners could not afford to retain counsel and just fretted.

Mrs. Perkins appeared oblivious to the whole thing.

Six months after the suit was filed, Garry paid a visit to each of the property owners. The homeowners were scared, and he was able to settle the claims against some of them for a relatively low sum. He did not care that the dispossessed families would end up living in some slum and ignored the pleas of wives and mothers who feared for the future of their loved ones. To him, this was just business.

The store and restaurant owners had been alerted that he was making the rounds and had their lawyer on the premises, who instructed them not to talk to Garry. The Baptist pastor received him politely, but after a while became irate at his demands and predicted that the wrath of God would soon descend on him.

Garry visited Mrs. Perkins last, even though hers was the plot that he had coveted from the beginning, since it fronted the highway. She seemed to be waiting for him, for her door opened just as he began rapping on it. "Hello, Mr. Flint," she greeted.

"Good afternoon, Mrs. Perkins. How are you getting on?"

"I am fine," she said curtly. "It has been years since I saw you last. What brings you to these parts?"

"I expect you know my business. We have brought legal action on behalf of the Johnson family to recover the estate that you and others have been unlawfully occupying for over a century. I have come to present you with an offer to settle your participation in the litigation."

"An offer, you say?" She sounded a little tentative, and Garry hoped that the last three years had taken a toll on her. She seemed even older and thinner, if possible, than during their first encounter. "I will listen to your offer, but first I would like to do a psychic reading of your aura, a little more extensive than last time."

"That won't be necessary," replied Garry. "I don't have time for fripperies today."

"In that case, sir, our meeting is over. The reading today would be for my benefit as well as yours. I must know if I can rely on whatever you have to say and trust any offer you may make." She opened the door to usher him out, but Garry sighed and did not move.

"Fine, let's do it your way. But please be quick about it."

"It won't take long. Please sit down."

Garry plunked down on the chaise lounge and offered his hands for the old lady's inspection. She sat on her chair, grasped his wrists with surprising force, and closed her eyes. A few minutes later she opened them with a start and looked at him, a deep frown on her face. "I have bad news for you, Mr. Flint."

"What do you mean?"

"Your aura has taken a steep turn for the worse."

"What do you mean?" he said again.

"Auras are transparent, even if multicolored. They reflect the psychic energy released by the chakras, but only absorb it when so much energy is given off that it has no place to go. As auras absorb energy they turn opaque, and it is no longer possible to discern the nature of the various emanations—that is to say, the thoughts and emotions that define a person at a given time. Your aura has turned almost completely opaque and seems to have been bombarded with negative energy."

"What do I care? That is a concern only to people like you who make a living reading, or pretending to read, them."

Mrs. Perkins's face broke into a joyless smile. "Not quite so. If an aura becomes totally opaque, it can no longer absorb the energy given off by the chakras and in some cases starts to bounce it back to the person's body. That may have bad physical consequences for the person."

"That's all poppycock," responded Garry, no longer able to contain himself.

"Perhaps. But the risk is all yours."

"Fine. Let's talk about my proposal."

"One more thing. You still have enough transparency left in your aura that I could, with some difficulty, look into the status of your physical health. You are in very bad shape. Instead of the pale green sheath that surrounds the aura of a healthy man, the sheath surrounding your aura is almost non-existent and the little that remains is almost white."

"Meaning?"

"You are killing yourself with what you do, and may not be around long to enjoy the fruits of your efforts."

"You let *me* worry about that, Mrs. Perkins. In the meantime, you know you are being sued and are likely to lose your property. Are you willing to compromise and let the Johnsons have it in exchange for a monetary payment? I can offer as much as a hundred thousand dollars in cash if you will give up your claims to ownership of this piece of land and move away."

"Never. Never. I said it to you years ago and I repeat it now. As long as I live, I am not moving out of this house or this land. Please be gone."

This time Garry stepped out the open door without hesitation. "We shall see about that," he mumbled as he departed.

* * *

By the time the fire engines arrived, the old clapboard house was engulfed by flames. Despite brave attempts by the firemen, the entire structure soon collapsed on itself and was reduced to a smoldering pile of half-consumed timbers.

When the heat abated sufficiently, a search of the ruins revealed the charred remains of an unrecognizable child or small old person. The cadaver was still holding close to its chest what appeared to be a large picture frame, unrecognizable but somewhat protected from the flames by the body of the person holding it.

Arson was suspected as the cause of the fire but could never be proved. If the fire that consumed Mrs. Perkins's home was set intentionally, this was done by professionals who knew their business.

Mrs. Perkins was ultimately determined to have died intestate, so the title to her home and the rest of her property passed to the State of Virginia. Garry, who by that time had managed to oust all but the Baptist pastor from the properties they formerly occupied, was able to use his influence to expedite the sale by auction of Mrs. Perkins's estate, which was purchased by Sally Johnson for a nominal amount since title to the property was under a cloud because of the litigation.

Garry's victory was now complete, and he wasted no time in launching an ambitious commercial development project that turned the Johnson Preserve into a multi-building complex that included offices, retail stores, and high-priced condos. Six years after he first drove by the clapboard home with the large sign in front, he had become a millionaire and was starting to consider retirement in some posh European spot.

So it was that one night he sat alone in his office, going over expansion plans for his project now that the Baptist Church had been finally evicted. He took to reflecting on all the efforts that had led to this moment, and for a fleeting instant felt something like regret over all the lives he had ruined, the people he had cheated, and even poor Mrs. Perkins's tragic but necessary end. But he quickly replaced those maudlin thoughts aside with a consoling one: *It was all worth it, because it is all mine now. Mine and no one else's.*

He poured himself another glass of brandy and was savoring the complex flavor and the aroma of the drink when he felt a piercing pain in his chest, as if it had been punctured by a sharp knife that left no blood but heat when it entered.

He tried to get up but perhaps he was too drunk or too weak to manage. He slid to the floor in front of his chair and passed out.

* * *

The coroner summarized his findings as follows:

"Mr. Flint was found on the floor of his office. His entire body was incinerated, save for the skull and a portion of each leg below the knee. The feet and legs were still clothed in socks and trousers, and his shoes were undamaged. The chair in which he had been sitting was partially destroyed.

"Investigation revealed that an unknown flame source charred his clothing at some location, probably near his chest or abdomen, splitting the skin and releasing subcutaneous fat, which was in turn absorbed into the burned clothing, acting as a wick. This combustion continued for as long as the fuel was available, which in the case of Mr. Flint was a long period of time, given that he was overweight and an alcoholic. The water in his body would have been the main impediment to combustion. However, slow combustion, lasting hours, gave the water time to evaporate slowly. The portion of the body that was found was totally desiccated.

"Mr. Flint's death is ruled 'death by burning,' whether from incineration or choking, since he had plainly inhaled the contents of his own combustion. Insufficient bodily remains were found, rendering it impossible to determine the exact cause or time of death."

THE MAGIC APPLE

"My name is Abú al-Sa'ádát.
I am the slave of this seal-ring,
standing in the service of him who possesses it.
Whatsoever he seeks I accomplish for him,
and I have no excuse in neglecting that he bids me do."
- Arabian Nights, "The Cobbler's Tale"

"Sir," said the merchant, giving it into his hand, "if you
look at the outside of this apple, it is very worthless, but if
you consider its properties, virtues, and the great use and
benefit it is to mankind, you will say it is no price for it,
and that he who possesses it is master of a great treasure.
In short, it cures all sick persons of the most mortal dis-
eases; and if the patient is dying it will recover him imme-
diately and restore him to perfect health."
- Arabian Nights,
"The Story of Prince Ahmed and the Fairy Paribanou"

1

"Sire, three more camels died overnight from lack
of food and water. Nobody is caring for them,
and no one is left to bury the carcasses."

Abu Ubaydah glowered at his aide-de-camp
and felt like striking him, but he restrained himself. "Forget
about the camels," he retorted. "How about the troops?"

"Since the start of the plague we have lost over five thousand soldiers, including archers and cavalrymen, as well as

scores of support personnel. We didn't have that many casualties in our great victory at the plains of Yarmouk two
years ago."

"I know," Ubayadah cut him off. "I mean how many
men have we lost since yesterday?"

"Actual deaths, two dozen or so. But so many of the sick
are in such poor condition that their death is all but certain."

"I fear we must leave Amwas. Caliph Umar, blessed be
his name, has been pressuring me to remove the army to a
more salubrious place, but I fear that we will carry the
plague with us wherever we go. Let's start getting ready.
We march to the highlands two days hence."

2

In the summer of the fateful Year of the Ashes, the Muslim troops in Syria abandoned their headquarters in Amwas
and relocated to the ancient city of Jabiya, in the Hauran
highlands. Many in the Muslim army died from the plague
during the exodus. Ubayadah was among those who perished.

The next three successors to Ubayadah also fell to the
plague in the months that followed. The position of commander of the Muslim forces in the Levant was rumored to
be accursed, and the next leader of the troops declined to
formally assume the title, though he was in effect in charge
of the army. His name was Zamar ibn Sakran.

3

"I'm by nature a cautious man," Zamar repeated to those
around him, this time his wazir, Abdur. "This plague knows
no rank or title and I feel as vulnerable to it as any of my
men. I need to make sure I don't get it."

"*Inshallah*," replied Abdur, "you are in no danger confined to your quarters. Every room is kept scrupulously

clean, and no filthy or unclean creatures can gain access to you. You are as safe from infection as we can make it."

"Yes, but…" Zamar drew breath shakily. "It's not only my fate that is at stake. The army I lead is ready to move west to redeem Egypt for the true faith. If I falter, who will lead them?"

"Caliph Umar has promised to send reinforcements" countered Abdur. "Perhaps other captains would be found—surely not as great as you but still capable of leading the true believers…" started the wazir.

"Never!" shouted Zamar. "*Insallah*, I must be the one in the lead."

And the argument ended there, only to be repeated soon thereafter.

4

Alas, despite all precautions, the plague caught up with Zamar. It started out with a fever that would not yield to cold compresses and baths in frigid water. The fever was accompanied by headaches and fatigue and all sorts of body aches. The second day, diarrhea and vomiting added to the symptoms.

Enough cases of the plague had run their course through the army that Zamar realized he was infected and in mortal danger. He summoned Abdur and demanded, in the tone of one used to being obeyed, "You must find a doctor who can arrest this curse. Don't come back unless accompanied by one."

Abdur knew his own life might be at stake, so he did not tarry. He sent messengers to all cities and villages within a hundred leagues of Jabiya, searching for word of miraculous cures for the fatal disease. Days went by, with no positive news.

Meanwhile, Zamar's condition continued to deteriorate. He developed boils on the groin and armpits. They were tender and hard to the touch; when Zamar ordered one of the nodules to be lanced, it discharged a loathsome fluid whose putrid smell lingered even after cleaning and dressing the wound.

The morning of the sixth day, Zamar was semi-conscious, beset by visions of taunting demons gathered around the bed where he lay. He felt death approaching and readied to render his soul to Allah the Merciful. He did not notice at first the arrival of two men: Abdur and a stranger dressed in black robes.

The sound of hushed voices brought Zamar back into reality. With an effort, he focused his blurred vision on the pair and recognized his wazir. "Abdur," he greeted feebly.

"Yes, sire." Abdur approached the bedside. "And with me is Ma'aruf bin Ka'b. He is a sorcerer who practices *sihr* in a small city south of here." Ma'aruf bent his head respectfully but remained silent.

Even on his deathbed, Zamar reacted sharply to this. "Sihr, and all forms of witchcraft, are condemned in the Quran. Why is he here?"

Abdur rushed to explain. "Sire, I found no practitioner of the healing arts who knows how to deal with the terrible plague that afflicts us. However, Ma'aruf here thinks he might be of assistance."

"How? I would not put my life and my immortal soul in the hands of a sorcerer!"

"With all respect, my lord, I would do nothing that would risk your life. What I propose may not work, but you wouldn't be any worse off for having tried it," offered Ma'aruf.

"So, what is your plan?"

"In the course of my studies I came across a *jinni*, a member of the unseen race of beings that are more than humans but less than angels. This jinni is not one of the malevolent ifrits of the jinn, but a kind spirit who has assisted me with many tasks and has made me rich and powerful. I propose that we summon him and see if he can get us a magical cure for your malady."

"Him?" cut in Abdur. "Do the jinn have sex?"

"Yes. Like humans, jinn can be male or female and can

procreate. In rare cases, a jinni can also have carnal knowledge of a human."

"What an abomination!" protested Zamar. "But how can you contact him?"

"I have him bound in a gold seal-ring which I always carry on my person." Ma'aruf proffered his left hand, on the middle finger of which sat an oversized ring covered with graven names, symbols, and wards. All I need to do to summon him is rub the center of the ring."

"Why don't you do it?" asked Zamar, who was beginning to lose consciousness.

"I shall presently do so. But first I must give you a warning."

"What's that?" interjected Abdur. "My master is dying; we have no time to waste."

"Abú al-Sa'ádát—that's the name of the jinni, though I call him just Abú—will obey any commands that would have him perform physical tasks. However, he is not bound to carry out any forbidden or abominable acts; such tasks he will decline to do altogether. He won't, for instance, re-awaken the dead or put a curse on a living person. Other tasks he may consent to do, but only as part of a bargain in which he is offered something he wants. Once I..."

From the bed came a croaking voice. "Never mind. Please hurry..."

5

Ma'aruf rubbed the center of the ring gingerly, and the room filled with a dense vapor that slowly condensed into a dark figure. What appeared before them was a vast shape, solid and yet not solid, vaguely human in the most horrible sense. It had twisted legs like a goat, one of them lower than the other. Huge genitalia hung from his naked body, which was covered with coarse hairs, and red vertical eyes gleamed fiercely in the middle of a misshapen head. His hands were oversized and had only four fingers, lacking thumbs. It stank of sulfur, filth, and corruption.

The apparition announced itself in a hollow voice that resounded like the wind inside a cave:

"I am Abú al-Sa'ádát. I am the slave of the seal-ring, standing in the service of him who possesses it. What can I do for you, Master?"

Ma'aruf responded with surprising familiarity. "Hail, Abú. I summon you today not on my own behalf, but that of my Lord Zamar ibn Sakran. As you can see, Lord Zamar is gravely ill and near death and there is no known cure in the human world for his malady. I call upon you to search in the hidden spheres for a boon—a magical remedy that will restore him to health."

Abú turned his fiery gaze upon the prostrate figure. "Human, I am not bound to render you any assistance. You do not hold the seal-ring and are not asking for matters of this world. Why should I help you?"

Zamar felt his last drops of energy dissipate. With a supreme effort, he replied, "I'm a Commander of the Faithful, on a mission to spread Allah's word throughout the world. If I die, His holy mission may not be accomplished. You must help me."

Abú shrugged. "The affairs of this world are of no concern to the jinn. You must deal with your problems without our help."

Zamar sunk into the mattress and began convulsing. Abdur called out to the servants outside the chamber. "Quick, bring some water to the Master!" Two terrified women came into the room carrying ewers of water and rags. They moistened the rags and gently dabbed the warrior's face. One of them brought an ewer to Zamar's lips, but he would not drink. After a while they retreated, weeping.

Zamar stopped shaking and became very quiet. Ma'aruf turned to Abdur. "Is he... dead?"

"I don't think so. He is frequently overcome by the fever and the deep distress of his body, but he is a very strong man and manages to rally. He may still be with us a bit longer."

A few moments later, Zamar opened his eyes again. In a

voice that was a mere whisper, he addressed the jinni. "What can I offer you? I have the ear of Caliph Umar, the most powerful and righteous ruler of the world. I can get you untold riches, beautiful palaces, vast domains, fame and honors. What would it take for you to agree to help me in my hour of need?"

"Human, the riches of the earth mean nothing to us jinn. We do not care for your palaces or your cultivated lands. We prefer deserts, ruins, and places of impurity like graveyards, garbage dumps, camel pastures—places where we can enjoy our solitude. And what fame and honor can you bestow on us, who are superior to humans in every way?"

Zamar fell into despair and had no more to say. At this point, Ma'aruf turned to his slave and asked, "Abú, are you married? In all the years of our association I've never heard you mention your wives or children."

The jinni could not fail to respond to a direct question from his master. "No, I am not."

"Why is that?"

The jinni waved his massive arms above his head as in lamentation. "The *jiniri*, the females of our kind, find me repulsive and will not couple with me."

Ma'aruf asked softly yet another question: "Would you like the company of a human female?"

Abú's response was a desolate groan. "I have never contemplated such a union. Yet, it is known that humans and jinn have gotten married and have had children as a result of their coupling."

Abdur cut in on the conversation. "Would you agree to help our lord if he can provide beautiful females for your pleasure?"

Abú would not answer Abdur's question but responded to it when it was posed again by Ma'aruf. "I have lived many hundreds of years and yearn for companionship, even from a human."

Abdur walked over to Zamar's bed and shook him back to consciousness. "Sire, would you be willing to offer human maidens to the jinni in exchange for his help?"

At first, Zamar did not understand Abdur's words through the fog that clouded his mind. Finally, the meaning of the query sunk in and he shook his head affirmatively. "Of course. How many slaves does he want?"

Abú responded directly to the dying man. In an offended tone, he replied, "I am sultan over two-and seventy tribes of the jinn, each two-and-seventy thousand in number, every one of which is under my command and may not gainsay me. I will not couple with a human slave. It would have to be a free maiden of high birth."

The jinni's words unwittingly brought to Zamar's mind the image of his favorite daughter, young Muunis. She had just turned sixteen and was exceptionally beautiful.

It is well known that the jinn can read human minds if they choose. Abú fixed his burning gaze inside Zamar's head and gasped. "*Yes!*" he roared. "It is *her* that I want!"

Ma'aruf and Abdur stood by uncomprehendingly, but Zamar uttered an animal shriek: "*No!* Not my daughter! *Never!*"

Perhaps had Zamar been less emphatic in his refusal, he might have been able to persuade the jinni to accept some other beauty of the many that graced the Caliphate. As it was, he must have hurt the jinni's already bruised pride, for he thundered back, "Human, refuse me and you will be gone before night falls. Give me your daughter in marriage or die!"

Everyone in the room blanched.

6

Ma'aruf was the first to recover. He faced the jinni sternly and commanded, "Abú! I order you to assist Lord Zamar without making ridiculous demands! We'll find a fair maiden to your taste anywhere in the world, but you must save this dying man!"

"Master, to find a cure for your lord will require the use of my magical powers. You know you can't order me to do this, and I refuse to do it unless he and I come to terms."

"Abú! I only need to rub this ring twice in quick succession and you will be consumed by the fire of the names graven on the ring. Obey me or you'll cease to exist."

"Do as you wish. I have lived a long life already. You shall not bend me to your will!"

The tense exchange was cut short by a sound from Zamar's bed. "I'll do it!" uttered Zamar in an agonized voice.

"Swear to it," shot back the jinni.

"I swear by Allah, the Most High. Cure me, and my daughter Muunis shall be yours."

"Your bargain is accepted. I shall return." With that, there was a dull sound like a candle snuffer putting out a flame and the jinni vanished.

7

"Where did that creature go?" asked Abdur, looking at the empty air that was filled by the jinni only seconds before.

"I don't know," replied Ma'aruf. "He usually seeks my leave before departing."

"I hope he gets back before it's too late." Abdur worriedly looked back at his master.

In just a few hours, Zamar's condition had deteriorated markedly. His skin showed signs of widespread, disseminated hemorrhage and necrosis; he was bleeding through every opening of his body and breathing with great difficulty. Death is at his door, concluded Abdur.

Ma'aruf was getting ready to depart when a noise at his back made him turn around. A cloud of dense fog had gathered at the foot of the bed where Zamar was at the point of expiring.

"I have returned," announced the hollow voice of the jinni. "And I have the cure your lord needs."

8

Abú held in his enormous hand an ordinary-looking apple; not too large, a little bruised, mostly red with an irregular yellow band around the stem. He brought the apple close to the face of the dying man, who inhaled its aroma and gasped.

"What are you doing?" asked Abdur, alarmed.

The jinni replied without turning away from the patient. "At the heart of one of the most desolate deserts in this world there is an oasis, graced by a magic stream. At the edge of its waters, a single apple tree grows. The apples from that tree are also magic. Their taste cures all sick persons of the most mortal diseases; even if the patient is dying, eating one of these apples will restore him to health."

"Will the apple you are holding make Lord Zamar well?" inquired Ma'aruf curiously, for this was a form of magic of which he was not aware.

"Yes, but not right away. He is too close to death and would not be able to eat the apple. But the very scent of the apple is magic and will stave off the progress of the disease and initiate recovery. I will return in three days to feed him the apple and start making arrangements for my betrothal to his daughter."

"Should we keep the apple here in case he is well enough that we can feed it to him?"

"That would not be wise," replied Abú. "If something were to happen to the apple before he consumes it, his recovery would be thwarted."

The jinni then vanished, again without seeking leave of his master.

9

When Abdur visited his commander early the following morning, he found Zamar awake and in somewhat better shape than the day before. He was no longer bleeding, and the necrosis was only visible on his toes and the fingers of his left hand. Yet, Zamar was still prey to high fever, chills, and retching in vain attempts to release the contents of his empty stomach.

Abdur proceeded to recount the events of the previous evening, which Zamar had missed for being unconscious. As Abdur mentioned that the jinni would return in three days to complete the cure and move ahead with the wedding, Zamar became agitated.

"Abdur, go find Ma'aruf right away, and have my daughter sent to me."

Muunis was even more beautiful in person than the image of her that Zamar had formed in his mind. Her skin was as white and unmarked as alabaster; her face was a perfect oval, framed by lustrous black hair that fell in a frozen cascade to the middle of her back. She had huge brown eyes, a small, straight nose, and a mouth as red as a ripe cherry. She moved with a poise that many dancers would have envied and deported herself with modesty and grace. This morning, though, Muunis was beset by worry. Dark circles under her eyes showed how little sleep she had enjoyed in the last few days.

"You called for me, Father? How are you doing?"

"A little better, my child. But it's not my health that I would like to discuss with you. Please bring cushions over beside the bed and sit near me, but not too close. We need to talk."

Muunis did as she was bid and sat facing her ravaged father.

"This loathsome disease will probably kill me, as it has thousands of my men," he started. He waved away an incipient protest by the girl and continued. "I want to live to serve Allah and my Caliph and spread the true faith throughout the land. I'm also fond of my existence and would like to remain alive for many more years, for the life of a conquering warrior has many rewards in fame and wealth." He paused to catch his breath and release a sigh of shame that was starting to choke him.

"For those reasons, noble and selfish, I did a terrible deed yesterday. While on the verge of death, I made a bargain with a loathsome creature, a jinni risen from the depths of the abyss. I promised, in exchange for his returning me to good health, to give your hand to him in marriage. The jinni accepted the bargain and is in the process of making me whole." He paused again, as the weight of these terrible words descended on his daughter like a crushing blow.

Muunis said nothing for a while, but the tears that streamed down her cheeks spoke volumes of her distress and she toppled, as if about to fall. At last, she braced herself against the edge of the bed for support and responded in a shaky voice, "You are my lord and master. Order, and I will obey." Her features froze into an expressionless mask.

Zamar watched as hopelessness took hold of his beloved daughter. He searched for words of consolation and could only come up with vague reassurances. "It's not all set yet. I may be able to find a way to save you from this fate."

As he continued to mumble, Muunis got up and walked away from her father, her shoulders heaving and her face twisted again by desolation and grief.

10

Zamar wasted no time on preliminaries when Abdur and Ma'aruf entered the sick room. "Sorcerer" he called out. "In your work, you deal frequently with the likes of the jinni that you brought here yesterday, and also with dangerous creatures like marids and ifrits and shaytans, isn't that so?"

"Yes, my lord. When you probe into the depths of the unseen, you risk calling forth malevolent beings that may wish to destroy you."

"How do you protect yourself against assaults from such beings?"

"Adepts of the hidden arts often fashion themselves an amulet, talisman or what is referred to as a *tawiz*, as protection against many forms of spiritual evil, including protection against the jinn. I have one such amulet, which I wear under my clothes around my neck." At this, Ma'aruf searched inside his tunic and brought out a round object the size of an egg, which dangled from a silver chain. He took it out and handed it to Zamar.

"The talisman typically contains, as does this one, a depiction of the Throne Room of Allah. It also has engraved secret words of power and the sacred names of our saints. For extra protection, in a small cavity in the center of the talisman I have dropped a few grains of pure sulfur mixed with tar. The smell of this mixture attracts and binds jinns, demons, and other fell creatures."

Zamar turned the rounded object this way and that and handed it back to the mage. "How difficult would it be to fashion one of these talismans?"

The question took Ma'aruf by surprise. "Not long, my lord. A skilled artisan under the supervision of an adept like me can get one finalized in a couple of days. Mind you, it would not be a work of art, since making fine engravings in a small object like this requires time and skill."

Zamar turned to Abdur and commanded, "Give this man a purse of silver." And then, to the sorcerer, "Ma'aruf, I want you to deliver into my hands two talismans like yours by tomorrow night, at the latest. See that you have these ready on time or you will face my displeasure."

Ma'aruf balked at the strange order. "My lord, I must warn you against taking any rash actions that you may later regret."

"Thanks for your concern, Ma'aruf. I'm well capable of protecting myself. Now, get to work on my assignment. See you no later than tomorrow night."

11

The sun was setting over the mountains that surrounded Jabiya when a breathless Ma'aruf made his entrance into the chambers where Zamar lay. The lord's condition had not changed in the last two days; he still was ravaged by fever, chills, and terrible pains. Despite his debility, Zamar raised himself on his elbows and greeted the sorcerer eagerly, "Do you bring me what I require?"

Ma'aruf inclined his head respectfully and, as he replied, "Yes, my lord," produced from his tunic two necklaces, identical in appearance, which he proceeded to present to the prone warrior, adding, "If I may say so, they turned out to be fine pieces of work."

Zamar inspected the talismans and questioned, somewhat dubiously, "And you are certain these will protect the wearers from attacks by the jinn?"

"Yes, my lord, they have saved me from harm a number of times. But why are you in fear of such an attack?"

"I will be meeting with your jinni tomorrow and want to be protected in case things don't turn out as they should."

"But why would they? You have entered into a bargain with Abú. He's not one of the malignant jinn, and will do nothing to attack you."

"Perhaps" replied Zamar. "In any case, I want you to come back tomorrow morning and stay with me until he comes." Turning to Abdur, he directed the wazir, "Take one of these talismans to Lady Muunis and ask her to put it around her neck and always keep it there."

"Your wish is my command."

12

It was late in the afternoon the following day, about the time the jinni had last appeared before the group. Abdur and Ma'aruf sat on divans near the bed where Zamar shifted restlessly. An expectant air filled the room as the three humans anxiously awaited Abú's arrival.

As in previous occasions, the air in the room suddenly became thick and darkened, to be filled, bit by bit, by the presence of the jinni. Abú finally materialized; he was carrying in one of his four-fingered hands the magic apple, which appeared small and inconsequential in the vast grasp of the creature.

The jinni addressed Zamar with unusual courtesy, "Greetings, Lord. I come to restore your health and banish the ills that afflict you." He came swiftly towards the bed and tendered the apple to the prone figure.

Zamar tried to reach for the fruit, but he was too weak, and his attempt failed midway to its target. As he sunk back into the mattress, Abú's monstrous face registered surprise followed by anger. "There is a smell in your body that draws me to it. I sense it also in my master sometimes." He then looked intently into Zamar's chest. "What is that? If I come closer, it will tear apart my essence!"

Zamar attempted again to reach for the apple, but Abú had already withdrawn to the far side of the room. "Foul human! You have betrayed me!"

Zamar attempted to explain. "We can't proceed with our bargain. My daughter shall not marry you. I was afraid you would react violently at the news."

"React? Do you think for a moment that I would dirty myself attacking a filthy human? *This* is my reaction!" His hand closed on the apple and squished it into nothingness.

Ma'aruf had been watching with sickening fascination as the deal between the jinni and the warrior unraveled. Now, fearing he was losing control over his slave, he shouted: "Abú! Abú al-Sa'ádát! I am your master, and command you to come forth and serve me!"

He was not getting an answer, so he rubbed the seal-ring time and again. There was a bright flash, a loud explosion and, all of a sudden, the room seemed empty again, save for three terrified humans.

13

Years passed. The plague was finally over, and the armies of Islam moved to occupy the near and far corners of Asia and Africa. The forces once stationed in Jabiya, now reduced to a few thousand survivors, were reinforced with fresh troops from Medina and went away to gain glories fighting Persians and Christians. Yet, in the now deserted headquarters of the Levant army, one house remained occupied but barely inhabited.

Muunis had never married and had become a bitter old woman, prematurely aged from cares and pain. Her life was simple: she kept house with the generous pension granted by the Calif, saw to her religious duties, and cared for her father.

Zamar was the last person on earth still afflicted by the plague. The disease would never go away, forever causing fevers, nausea, diarrhea, and pain. Zamar and his daughter, separately and at times together, prayed to Merciful Allah to end the old warrior's life and thus his suffering. But all the cells in his body, once reinvigorated by the scent of the magic apple, refused to die, clinging to the blind hope that soon the juice of an otherworldly fruit would render them healthy again.

THE PORTAL

My object all sublime / I shall achieve in time —
To let the punishment fit the crime — /
The punishment fit the crime;
And make each prisoner pent / Unwillingly represent
A source of innocent merriment! / Of innocent merriment!
- Gilbert and Sullivan, *The Mikado*, Act 2

So far, the crowning point of my career as a Middle Eastern Studies scholar had been the release by Screeching Owl, Ltd. of my treatise, *The Great Old Ones and Others—The Lost History of the Ancient Deities.*

Screeching Owl was reluctant to take on publishing a six-hundred-page tome on the stories and myths surrounding the powerful deities from space that once ruled the Earth and have since fallen into a deep sleep. "There is no market for that kind of crap," an editor proclaimed.

I was able to convince him and others at the firm that there *is* a market for this esoteric area of scholarship by citing novels, movies, short stories, and even Ph.D. dissertations dealing with the topic. I told them a good number of people dread the possibility that ancient monsters might just be waiting for a chance to return to reclaim the planet. In short, I overwhelmed their opposition with facts, figures, and sales projections.

I was soon proved right: announcement of the impending release of my book in the trade press was followed by a healthy number of pre-publication orders; four months later, Amazon sales upon release of the work exceeded even the rosiest predictions of the publishers.

* * *

At the end of the quarter, I was awaiting my first royalty payment. Since Screeching Owl was headquartered in London and I lived in rural New Mexico, payments would occur via SurePay, a multi-national company operating an online payment system that handles money transfers between consumers and merchants, and also among business entities. The use of a middleman like SurePay was far more convenient and secure than payment by check or other forms of money exchange.

Thus, in the afternoon of last December 31, I received notice that a royalty payment of $1,753.88 had come from Screeching Owl, and was told that I should sign onto my SurePay account to claim it. I became very excited, beaming with pride at my wife. "My first royalties from the book on the Old Gods have arrived!" She had been skeptical of the economic value of my research and writing of the book, so the money would also settle in my favor this dispute between us. But, more importantly, I could really use the money. I was a non-tenured college professor who specialized in an obscure branch of learning. Even in a remote corner of a less-than-prosperous state, life was expensive and we lived hand to mouth, like many Americans do these days. My mortgage payment was due in a week.

So, I checked my SurePay account, looking for the money that I would immediately direct to my bank account in Las Cruces. The money was not there. I tried multiple times over the course of the day to no avail.

Because of the time difference, it was already New Year's Day in London, and all businesses were closed. I could not get hold of anybody and was not about to pester my editor in the middle of the night; there was nothing she could do, in any case.

It was nine hours earlier in New Mexico than in London, but midnight was also approaching here. While everyone else was drinking and partying, I spent the last hours of the year trying to figure out how to get hold of my money.

*　*　*

When I signed in to my SurePay account online, I was offered three help choices: go to the resolution center; ask for "community help;" and go to the message center and attempt to communicate by e-mail with someone. I tried all three. The advice from the "resolution center" would help only if I was disputing a transaction; here there was no transaction and nothing to dispute. The "community help" recommendation was to suggest that if I had not received an amount due because of a mistake, I should correct the mistake and try again; this I could not do, because I was not sure there was a mistake and, in any event, it was not my error but someone else's. Finally, the message center just raised all kinds of potential issues and offered suggested solutions. I kept asking to be transferred to a representative, and instead of complying, the site software kept demanding that I answer questions about my problem and suggesting inapplicable fixes. I kept calling for "customer service" and later pleaded "Human, human, human, I want to speak with a human!" After an eternity and numerous tries, I was offered the option of sending a message describing my issue but warning that representatives would be available only during business hours and responses would be slow at times of high traffic. Thus, the first opportunity for a customer service contact would be nine a.m. during working days. Since New Year's fell on a Friday, that meant there would be nobody to help me until Monday.

Disheartened, I went to bed at three a.m., having missed all the New Year's celebrations.

I was in a sullen mood on Saturday but contacted my editor right after I got up. She was at work and was able to look at the record of the royalty payment. "Yes, we transferred the money to your SurePay account Thursday evening, just before we closed shop."

"Let's double-check something. To what account did you direct the transfer?"

"Why, to your Oldgods1$@gmail.com account."

"Oh, you must have forgotten that I had to open a new account because of the hacking incident in November. It's now Newgods1$@gmail.com."

There was an embarrassed silence on the line. Then, "Let me see if I can get that transfer canceled or redirected to you."

"I'll keep doing the same," I promised. "First one who gets this problem solved should tell the other right away."

* * *

Monday went by, and then Tuesday and Wednesday. I kept getting no response to my requests to speak to someone. The tone and content of my monologue with the computer turned more irritated and ultimately became abusive. I was on the line frequently with the editor, who was equally frustrated at her failure to connect with anyone. Finally, late Thursday evening, as I was getting ready for bed, three miraculous little dots appeared on the previously blank screen of my laptop and someone typed in: "*Hello. This is Andrea. How can I help you?*"

I was so shocked that I almost did not respond, but finally gathered my wits and explained, "*In the transaction that I identified in earlier messages, the merchant sent me a seventeen-hundred-and-fifty-dollar payment, only it was sent to the wrong account.*"

"*Do you know the account to which it was sent?*"

"*Yes.*"

"*Do you have an e-mail account under that name?*"

"*No, but I can create one right away.*"

"*Please do that. I will open a new SurePay account for you under the new name. The money will appear on that account when you sign into it.*"

Ten minutes later, the royalty payment was on its way to my bank.

* * *

A lot had happened in the intervening week. The failure of the royalty transfer had prevented me from paying two credit card balances, resulting in the imposition of late charges and a drop in my credit rating. Automatic payments to a couple of utility and internet service providers had failed, causing my accounts to be threatened with suspension. My wife was increasingly mad at the dereliction of my head of household duties and refused to cook for us, forcing upon me the indignity of eating at fast-food Mexican restaurants. I had lost sleep, my blood pressure had risen to stratospheric levels, and the lack of an outlet for my anger was surely shortening my life.

I shared my frustration with the Screeching Owl editor, and she was sympathetic to my complaints but unhelpful. "That's the way the world runs these days. Anyone with power over even a small corner of the Internet can lord over you."

I was too upset to concede she had a valid point. Instead, I persisted. "I want revenge. There must be something I can do to get back at those bastards."

There was a brief silence, and I could almost hear the wheels inside her brain turning. "Well," she finally said. "Aren't you the world's leading expert on the Great Old Ones?"

"Yes, but..."

"Why don't you enlist their help in getting you satisfaction?"

It was perhaps intended as a throwaway remark, but it got me thinking.

* * *

Opening a portal to the realm outside time where the Old Ones are confined was not that difficult for an expert like me. Without getting into boring details, all that was needed was a supply of each of the four elements (wind was hardest to get; I had to fish out a desktop fan from the days before air conditioning); white chalk, to draw a pentagram within a large circle of the floor of the attic; many lit black candles for atmosphere; and some knowledge of Akkadian, the ancient language of Assyria and Babylon. I positioned myself outside the circle, extinguished all extraneous lights, and recited an invocation from a version of the Tablet of Destinies I had found in a Baghdad museum.

I had to try the invocation four times, more and more loudly, until a vague form of dun-colored mist began to materialize in the pentagram. Even before fully forming, the presence made itself known. "Stop that racket, will ye? It's quite annoying." This, in English with a decidedly Jersey Shore accent.

I had expected to summon a vast, threatening ghost like the jinni that appeared before Aladdin in *The Arabian Nights*. I was ready to cower, prostrate myself, and beg for the apparition's indulgence. No need. What came out into the circle was a misshapen, gray, hairless little figure with an oversized head, small, beady eyes gleaming with malice, twisted limbs, and oversized claws. It was naked and of indeterminate sex and seemed more pitiful than awe inspiring.

"Who... who are you?" I questioned, half in fear, but at the same time fighting to refrain from tittering.

"My name is Bingaith. I'm one of the countless spawns of Shub-Niggurath, the Mother of all."

"Are you *really* one of the Great Old Ones?" I questioned, indelicately suggesting doubt.

"You mortals are always classifying things. I'm great enough," Bingaith replied, a bit peevishly.

"O, Great One, pardon my ignorance!" I was quick to abash myself. "I summoned you to seek assistance on a grave matter."

"I'll decide whether your matter is grave and warrants my intervention. And I will set my price if I deign to help you."

I described my grievances against SurePay and my generalized anger at how modern society has made people enslave themselves to machines so they can spend more time watching stupefying tripe in front of their television sets.

Bingaith listened to my tirade without registering any reaction. However, when I ran out of steam he commented, "I'm familiar with your problems. I learned English watching *The Real Housewives of New Jersey*. I can tell you that early on, when humans were barely above the level of apes, things were simpler, and people were closer to the demands of their genetic imprint. Hunting, eating, mating, and not getting killed by a predator were the main preoccupations of those of your kind. You have perverted what Nature intended for your species and gotten yourselves in all sorts of trouble. Why should I help you with your self-inflicted difficulties?"

I replied tartly, "I don't understand why you are so picky. From all I've read, those of your kind were utterly defeated in a war that took place eons ago and are imprisoned in a frozen hell outside time and space. You linger there hoping to come back one day to rule the Earth. I have brought you back and given you a chance to open the door to the Old Ones so they can return. Why are you reluctant to venture in?"

Bingaith's response was full of undisguised contempt. "The bonds that tied us have loosened with time. We can return to this planet, as we have done to many others, any day we want, provided we are extended a proper invitation. The question is, why would we want to rule a dump of a world on the verge of ruin?"

"Perhaps things are less dire than you believe. Maybe you should get a better understanding of the modern world before giving us the back of your hand."

Bingaith stared at me fixedly, exuding evil from his loathsome features. "All right. I'll do as you ask. I'll wreak havoc on that company against which you hold a grudge. But if returning to this world is not to my liking, I'll come back to collect from you. In blood."

* * *

Several days went by. I waited anxiously for news of the destruction of the SurePay headquarters that Bingaith had promised. Surely, a catastrophic event of that nature would have been all over the news media. But there was silence.

I refused to believe that even a minor Old deity would renege on his commitments. When the suspense proved too great to endure, I conducted another summoning. Again, I had to repeat the words of the incantation several times before getting a response, but this time, what materialized in the portal was quite a different figure.

Bingaith was no longer naked but was dressed in a three-piece pinstriped suit with a white shirt and a silk power tie. He was outfitted with Louboutin dress shoes and wore enormous Giorgio Armani sunglasses that covered most of his hideous face. The claws had been carefully manicured, and what could be seen of his skin appeared suntanned.

"What do you want now?" was his harsh greeting.

Trying not to sound irritated, I responded, "I was wondering when you are going to make good on the promise you made about SurePay."

Bingaith opened his mouth in a horrible imitation of a smile that displayed all his sharp teeth. "Clearly, you don't get news here in the boondocks. It was done three days ago."

"Come on, the destruction of the headquarters of a big Silicon Valley company would have been in all the newspapers."

Bingaith's attempt at a smile became even more horrible as it grew wider. "Who said I promised that the company headquarters would be destroyed? That was your idea, not mine."

"So, what did you do instead?" I almost shouted.

"Well, being from the area around Babylon and such, I had never made it to California. It is really very nice out there. I like it."

"And?"

"Here, this will explain everything to you." Bingaith produced a piece of paper from the inner pocket of his jacket and handed it to me. Its heading read: "*SurePay announces reorganization, outlines plans to increase profitability.*" Below was a summary of a press release:

SurePay (Nasdaq SUPY) announced last night a complete revamping of its management team and an ambitious plan to streamline its money-transferring services. All members of the board of directors and the company's upper management have agreed to resign; each one is to receive a bonus payment in the tens of millions of dollars. In their place, a new board and executive team have taken over the management of the multi-billion-dollar company. At the helm of the new team is Rashid Ahmed Bingaith, a native of the United Arab Emirates and a graduate of the Wharton Business School.

In a conference call with the business press, Mr. Bingaith announced plans for a drastic reduction of personnel at SurePay's offices, with the goal of making the company's services nearly 100% automated. "The human element has been the main source of inefficiency in our operations. Our aim is to have our services provided by state-of-the art, proven software that will make monetary transfers even faster and more reliable than they are today," said Mr. Bingaith…

I stopped reading. "What did you do to the old managers of SurePay?" I didn't really want to know but felt compelled to ask.

"Why, we ate them," chortled Bingaith, as a viscid tongue flickered in and out his mouth. "And then we replaced them with some of my brothers, which I brought over through your portal."

I became a little nervous. "Where does that leave me?"

"You have nothing to fear. I am extending you

professional courtesy. After all, it was your idea that got us involved again in human affairs. By the way, I am starting to convince others among the Old Gods that it is time for them to make their comeback to Earth, and that corporate takeover is a much better way for them to rule than through carnage."

"Does that mean that I will have to summon each Old God who wishes to re-enter our planet?'

"No. As long as the original portal remains intact, they may come and go freely without your involvement. But I have to go now. I have a company to run."

* * *

A week afterward, my attic had become the Grand Central Station of Old Gods traffic. The comings and goings were frequent and noisy enough that we had to cordon off the portion of the family room that lay beneath the attic and give up use of the entertainment center. My wife was increasingly livid; I had explained to her that I was running a delicate experiment in the attic and the commotions would soon cease, but she was not assuaged.

Then some recently reorganized companies began attempting to acquire each other in a series of wild proxy fights between factions of the Old Gods. I no longer dared enter the family room since some of the raucous sounds coming out of the attic above were bloodcurdling.

I became tempted to move to a nearby motel for fear that the fights would spill to other parts of the house and would impact us. However, I was concerned that abandonment of the premises might cause the portal to collapse and direct the ire of the deities against us, so I did nothing. But after weeks of ceaseless turmoil, I judged that I had to do something to at least clarify our situation.

I tiptoed into the attic one mid-afternoon, usually the quietest time for otherworldly appearances. The room was eerily quiet. I started going through the invocation routine and was in the middle of my recitation from the Tablet of

Destinies when there was a rush of hot air and Bingaith materialized in the pentagram.

His looks had worsened since our last encounter. He was naked, like the first time we met, and exhibited what appeared to be burn marks, missing chunks of anatomy, and other signs of physical distress.

I could not contain my amazement, and again asked an indelicate question, "Bingaith, you look like hell. What happened to you?"

Bingaith snapped his teeth in an attempt to take a bite off my body. I jumped behind a recliner and found myself apologizing again to the little monster.

"A million pardons; I didn't mean to criticize. But you are not wearing fancy clothes or designer dark glasses. I was merely noting the change."

"Mortal, watch your every word. I must come when you summon me, but that doesn't mean I have to be nice to you."

"Oh, you are always nice to me," I replied hypocritically.

"Okay, stop the bull. Why have you forced me back?"

I came clean with my misgivings. "I was happy to see how you fixed my grievance with SurePay and just as glad that you took care of several other corporate malefactors. But then I have been reading accounts that suggest you guys are going at each other, and that concerns me. Where is it all going to end? And what's going to happen to us mortals?"

Bingaith seemed to be ready to jump at me again but restrained himself. "The Old Gods had been away from this planet for so long that we had forgotten how nice things can be around here. Earth is, for the most part, beautiful, and you monkeys are easy to manipulate and control, and are tasty snacks to boot.

"I made a bad mistake. As more among us came over through the portal at my suggestion, there was an increased appreciation for how pleasant life can be in this corner of creation. And that was the problem: there are too many of us and too little Earth to enjoy. Our kind doesn't like to share, we prefer to overcome others by force and consume all who challenge us.

"So, we have been fighting with each other for dominance over the world. And as is the case with the human nations, some of us are stronger than others, and after a while, the weaker ones have been disposed of, and what's left are several factions of what you would call super-powers.

"Alas, the spawns of Shub-Niggurath are not the greatest of the Old Ones. We had the advantage of getting here first, but since then several of the mightiest Old Gods have come through the portal: Baoht Z'uqqa-Mogg, Cthulhu, his sister Cthaeghya, Gisguth, and others. I and my team were eliminated in the first round of the fight, but the battles among the strongest Old Ones continue."

Bingaith fell silent. I waited a bit to see if he would resume his tale, but he seemed to have run out of steam. So, I asked still another indelicate question:

"What happened to you then?"

This time Bingaith was able to get a hold of my shirt and began pulling me toward him. I clung to the arms of the recliner and fought for dear life to avoid being consumed. At length, Bingaith appeared to calm down. He let go of my shirt and continued.

"We losers are confined back in the prison outside time from which we had escaped. But now we are watched by our siblings to ensure we do not try to make a comeback."

"Does that mean that the more powerful of the Old Ones will continue to make war on each other?"

"Yes, and sometime soon they will turn against humans openly and enslave them all."

"Will we ever get relief from this plague?" It felt hopeless.

"You will get a bit of relief from us each month. The Old Ones must return to their place of captivity for one night and one day, at the rising of the full moon. We use that time to settle scores, resolve grievances, and plan future forays into other worlds."

"Every month?"

"Yeah. Like eight days from now, when the full moon

returns. You will get a quiet day then. Enjoy it."

* * *

I agonized day and night over the Old Gods problem, and in the course of a week, I developed a plan and got ready to carry it out. By the early afternoon of the day the full moon was to rise, I had bought (paying cash) a large container of chlordane, a highly flammable insecticide, at a lawn care store. I filled every corner of the attic with chlordane-soaked rags, tied to each other by a thin strip of cloth soaked with chlordane that would serve as the trigger. I did not use gasoline because chlordane is odorless, whereas the smell of gasoline could give the game away. I sprinkled the rest of the chlordane into the fireplace to increase the combustion potential.

I went to bed as usual but did not sleep. I got up carefully, making sure not to wake up my wife, and stared in silence out of the kitchen window until the full spring moon rose into the heavens.

After waiting a few minutes out of caution, I climbed the stairs to the attic and opened the door to a welcome, silent darkness. I took out a book of matches, lit a match to the strip of cloth, closed the attic door, and ran downstairs as fast as my legs would carry me.

I was out of breath when I reached the bedroom, and the breathlessness lent credibility to my voice when I screamed at my sleeping wife, "*Fire! Fire! The house is on fire! We need to get out!*"

We barely had time to clear the front door, half naked, as blinding flames and smoke erupted out of the attic and moved quickly through the clapboard house. We were shivering with cold and shock when the fire brigade arrived. They handed us blankets and cups of steaming coffee to get warm as we watched the firemen fight in vain to save the house from the engulfing fire.

* * *

The insurance company investigators had trouble reaching a conclusion as to the cause of the fire. On the one hand, they found a couple of partially consumed rags in the ruins of the attic. Those might or might not have been soaked with something, but that something had evaporated. There were also a number of strange things strewn around, including gardening soil, a large vat that had contained water, and a charred vintage fan. On the other hand, the house was not worth much and the insurance recovery would go mainly to the mortgage company. Their investigation of my affairs showed that I was a renowned scholar, in no financial trouble.

In the end, they paid off a couple of hundred thousand dollars for the house and its contents. I dickered over my share of the settlement proceeds but pocketed the small payment that was due us. I never had thought that I could someday make money out of committing arson.

*　*　*

This all happened six months ago. In that period, I wrote a sequel to my treatise, this time a semi-fictional narrative entitled *Conversations with the Old Ones*. I did not mention Bingaith by name and advanced the concept that, contrary to popular belief, the world would take a turn for the worse if the Old Ones came back to restore order. Screeching Owl literally tore the manuscript out of my hands and published it in record time. It is now number four in the New York Times nonfiction bestsellers list.

My wife and I have found a new source of discord: what to do with the insurance proceeds and the royalties we are getting. We'll probably end up buying a condo in Taos, as far from our former abode as we can get without leaving New Mexico.

I would have gladly accepted the loss of all my possessions as just punishment for past misdeeds. It would have been worth it to end up penniless, just to make sure that the portal for the migration of Old Ones into this world was closed.

My contract with Screeching Owl requires that all royalty payments be made by direct bank-to-bank transfer. I reckon that banks are safe, at least for the time being. Although these days one never knows.

THE COMPLETE *TURANDOT*

La tua anima è in alto!
Ma il tuo corpo è vicino.
Con le mani brucianti stringerò i lembi d'oro del tuo
manto stellato…
La mia bocca fremente premerò su di te…
- Giacomo Puccini, *Turandot*, Act III

I

You could call me a grave robber and you would not be far off the mark. I would take exception only to the notion that I have stolen a dead man's possessions: I was only after his thoughts and ideas, nothing material. But a grave robber I was all the same.

It all started with my love for music. My parents had season tickets to the Met and attended several performances each year. They began taking me when I was eight and I soon developed a taste for opera and some familiarity with the operatic repertory. I was enthralled by the beautiful music, the dancing, the stagecraft, and the outright showmanship in many of the shows. I remember leaning over the railing in front of my second balcony seat, watching with rapt attention as down, miles below, the works of Verdi or Wagner unfolded.

Puccini's *Turandot* was a particular favorite of mine. I loved its Oriental sonorities that highlighted the fairy tale plot, and the beautiful arias through which the story unfolded. Yet the last few minutes of the opera always left me unsatisfied; what should have been a climactic love duet actually came across as an unimaginative repetition of passages from earlier moments in the opera.

There was a reason for my dissatisfaction. Puccini had died in November 1924, leaving the last two scenes of *Turandot* unwritten. The opera was completed by Franco Alfano, a minor composer who used melodies from earlier parts of the work to finish the score. While this proved an adequate solution, the love duet at the end of the opera was missing the soaring melodies that Puccini was capable of generating.

I was frustrated, as many others had been before me, by the loss of the composer's final expression of this talent, and was determined to do something about it someday, though I didn't know what.

II

From an early age, my parents tried to steer me toward a profitable career in science or technology, but my mind reveled in the fantasies that artists, particularly composers, had created over the ages. The struggle ended when it was discovered that I had perfect pitch and considerable musical aptitude. I was enrolled in a conservatory and became a professional pianist, and later, the musical director and main conductor of a midwestern opera company. By the age of forty-five, I was moderately successful but wasn't blazing any trails.

It was midway through my fifth season as a conductor that I had a mid-life crisis of sorts. The opera company was always struggling with a lack of money, and I had to spend many of my working hours trying to squeeze donations out of wealthy patrons and indifferent corporate sponsors. Because of budget limitations, I was able only to schedule works that called for small casts and posed modest staging demands. No *Aida*s with elephants marching across the stage, no monumental Ring cycles for our company. It was professionally unsatisfying and left me feeling I was in a rut from which I saw no way of disengaging myself.

I had to do something. I needed a project that could bring me worldwide recognition. And then I thought of the lost finale of *Turandot*. What if I could somehow find the missing music? If I could perform for the first time *the complete Turandot*, fame would surely follow.

I researched. In early 1924, *Turandot* was almost finished. The premiere was planned for the following April. Puccini was suffering from throat cancer and traveled to Brussels for treatment. He took with him, all sketched out, the missing final scenes of *Turandot*.

He never had a chance to complete his opera. The treatment—involving radioactive needles and a tracheotomy—was severe. After three weeks, he suffered a fatal heart attack.

Surely, I concluded, Puccini must have had the final scenes of the opera in mind right up to the moment of his death. If only those thoughts could be retrieved...

Then I read an article that reported that brain cells can stay alive and function for a while even after we're clinically dead, before finally flickering out. In particular, genes in the neural cells responsible for brain functions like thought and memory may stay active for up to twelve hours or more after death. This discovery did not help me directly but suggested that if I could somehow communicate with the dead Puccini he would have "fresh" in his mind the music from *Turandot* that never saw the light of day.

But communicating with a dead person would involve seeking the assistance of a medium or engaging in necromancy. I immediately discarded mediums as charlatans who preyed on the ignorant and the weak—the stereotypical spinster trying to get in touch with her dead poodle. Necromancy, however, was once considered a reputable science that enabled its practitioners to manipulate death and bring back the "shadow" of the dead, and perhaps use those conversations to their advantage. Alas, necromancy had been almost entirely extinguished after the Renaissance, and finding anyone who could impart its secrets on me was nearly impossible.

III

After much investigating, I heard—in a chat room where a bogus form of necromancy was being discussed as part of a role-playing game—of the possible existence of a real living necromancer. The person who provided the tip explained that she used to live in Bucharest as a student and would go to the countryside on excursions. On one of those trips, she visited a village known as Corabia on the shores of the Danube. There, over dinner at a local inn, she overheard a conversation concerning a Mrs. Draganu, a magician who could summon the dead and talk to them. She never actually met Mrs. Draganu, but by talking to several people in the village she was able to confirm the local reputation of the lady in question as adept in communicating with deceased people.

I found no information on Mrs. Draganu on social media. I contacted the Romanian embassy, and they suggested that I send a letter to her in an envelope addressed to the Corabian postmaster, with a note that solicited his help with locating the lady in question. I don't speak Romanian, but I found a college student who agreed to write a letter to Mrs. Draganu and translate the answer for me, should there be one.

Several weeks went by. I had almost forgotten my attempt to communicate with a peasant lady in the Balkans when I received a letter from Romania with a return address in Corabia. The letter was written in French, and in it, Mrs. Draganu informed me that yes, she was a necromancer who had learned the art from her grandmother and now used it mainly to communicate with her deceased husband. She was willing to take me as a pupil, but I would have to travel to Corabia and lodge with her since there were no hotels or inns in town. She quoted me a ridiculously low charge for her services and suggested that I come in the summer, when the weather was better than during other seasons.

I was a bachelor and had no commitments during the summer since the opera was idle then. I immediately responded to her and tentatively set our meeting for the upcoming summer, three months away.

IV

That summer and the following one, I traveled to a small village in Southwest Romania, where one of the last practitioners of the ancient art of necromancy still plied her trade. After two seasons of intensive training, I reached a level of proficiency that allowed me, most of the time, to summon Mrs. Draganu's dead husband—a teacher with whom I was able to hold halting but relatively pleasant conversations in French.

To cast a necromantic spell, there is first a need for reagents, which are natural materials that are used up during the incantation process. These must be placed within an empty bag, which then must be closed. After this, the necromancer must place a Key of the Caretaker (a metal pin with a small fake skull on the top) upon the bag to channel the energy of the cosmos into the bag. The necromancer will speak words of power and the reagents will be consumed, to be replaced by a spell talisman inside the bag. The talisman will remain in the bag, waiting for the spell to be cast.

I intended to cast the "Death Speak" spell, which allows the caster to have a single, brief conversation with a deceased person. It is a fairly straightforward spell but requires the necromancer to be in physical contact with the body of the deceased. Thus, I needed to travel to Italy and visit Puccini's tomb to be able to speak with him.

The body of Puccini is buried with that of his wife and

son in a mausoleum inside the villa where he used to live, which overlooks Lake Massaciuccoli, a lake on the Apuan Alps. The closest town to the villa is Torre del Lago Puccini, a small community about fifteen miles from Lucca. The villa is open for tours, which include the mausoleum itself. The home of Puccini, a world-famous composer whose music is beloved by millions of people throughout the world, is the frequent target of tours that start from Torre del Lago Puccini and include a visit to Puccini's villa.

I studied the tour brochures and discovered that, in the winter months, tours are held only three days a week, Thursday through Saturdays, and tours ended at five p.m. Armed with that information, I arranged to travel to Italy on a Friday in March, leaving the opera performances that weekend in the hands of my assistant. I intended to carry out my task over the weekend and be back home by the following midweek.

V

I arrived in Lucca on a Saturday morning, rented a car, and drove to Torre del Lago Puccini, where I had reserved a room for two nights at a bed and breakfast hotel near Puccini's villa. I would depart Monday morning at the latest.

That evening, right after sunset, I went over on foot to Puccini's villa. A cold rain was falling steadily, and I got drenched during the short walk. The gate was locked, but I picked the lock with large pliers I had bought for that purpose in Lucca. I opened the gate slowly, careful to make no noise, and headed in the darkness towards the mausoleum, which is located in the gardens adjacent to the main building. Because of the heavy rain, the darkness, and the detached location of the mausoleum, there was little chance that the caretakers would observe an intruder approaching it.

The door to the mausoleum was closed, but not locked. I

entered the structure, turned on a flashlight, and proceeded to the little chapel where Puccini's casket lay, sitting on an ebony pedestal in the center of the building. I was ready to get to work.

The casket's lid had been secured by turning a sealing key, and I had purchased a casket key from a funeral home. Turning my key in a hole at the foot of the coffin, I was able to unlock the lid, lift it, and lower it carefully onto the floor adjacent tp the platform where the coffin lay.

I had already chosen my reagents—a lamb bone and a thimble of my own blood—and had placed them inside a closed bag. I spoke the words of the Death Speak incantation that transformed the reagents into a talisman that provided the link that allowed me to have a conversation with the deceased.

VI

The air filled with a nauseating stench as the remains of Puccini became exposed after a century of rest. To my surprise, the cadaver's skeleton was hardly visible; cornification had occurred over most of the body, leading to the deposition of a thin layer of repulsive yellowish material over the remains. I had to be in physical contact with the corpse for the duration of the spell while concentrating deeply on the question I wanted to pose. However, laying a gloved hand on the layer of corruption that covered the corpse elicited an almost unbearable revulsion, and I was only able to restrain myself from vomiting or drawing away from the corpse through the full exercise of my will.

I am not a powerful necromancer but only a barely competent one, so I was able to ask only one question. I had thought about and rehearsed the question, and now posed it in a trembling voice while holding the bag with the talisman above the corpse:

"Puccini, at the moment of your death you were composing the finale of your last opera, *Turandot*, but were unable to commit the music to paper. Sing for me the final love duet between Calaf and the Princess."

There was a long silence, underscored by the pelting of the rain against to outside walls of the mausoleum. Then a broken voice, made of sound shards rather than complete words, responded to my request with a harsh question of its own:

"Who dares disturb a resting soul to ask such a mundane question?"

I was terrified by the unexpected question from the composer and began shaking uncontrollably. Yet I managed to frame an insincere reply. "The entire world wants to know. With that duet, *Turandot* would be the greatest opera ever written."

An even angrier response awaited me. "I don't want to sing for you, and you can't make me."

Since my appeal to the vanity of a long-dead man had failed to carry the day, I felt I had to apply brute force. I placed the bag with the talisman on the cadaver's midriff, which started smoking. Then I shouted at the top of my voice, "Giacomo Puccini, I command you to sing that duet for me!"

There was an audible growl coming from deep within the corpse. After a pause, a distorted but recognizable melody began to resonate against the walls of the mausoleum. I extracted from my coat pocket a wad of lined music paper and a fountain pen and hurried up to catch the musical phrases. I knew Giuseppe Adami and Renato Simoni's libretto by heart, so I could follow who was singing what words in a given moment, though often the sound was so muddled to be almost unrecognizable.

After five agonizing minutes, the otherworldly voice stopped and I looked at what I had transcribed. It was of course magnificent. An entirely new set of counterpointing melodies not previously heard in the opera or anywhere else, and written by Puccini, for that matter. I pressed the sheaves of paper to my chest and exhaled in relief.

I let go of the putrescent arm of the corpse and got to my feet, starting to gather my belongings. It was then that a blinding light illuminated the scene, followed by the sound of a thousand cracking whips. Seconds later, there was a brutal crash as something shook the entire mausoleum.

VII

I didn't know what had happened, but instinct told me to run away from the horror. I ran to the door, turned the handle, and tried to swing it out. The door didn't budge.

I tried pushing the door with my hand, then with my shoulder, then with my entire body. The door didn't move an inch. Something large and heavy was resisting my efforts. A fallen tree? A rock? I kept hitting the door with all I had—even the coffin lid—to no effect.

It was Saturday night. Nobody would come this way for hours, if not days. There would be no tours of the Torre di Lago until midweek. My apartment was rented until Monday and might not be visited by the owners before then. If the caretaker failed to notice the obstructed door, there might be no rescue for quite a while.

The air in the mausoleum was already feeling thick. I shivered, although the temperature inside the closed building was rising. I felt I was asphyxiating already.

I sat, leaning against a door that wouldn't move, my breaths getting shorter as I panicked. Perhaps I was getting delirious; I seemed to hear a presence, maybe a distant voice, uttering mocking words. Had Puccini brought about my entrapment in his tomb?

My heart raced and I felt a sharp stab of pain in my chest. I became faint and passed out.

VIII

They found me later, after the caretaker saw the trunk of

a large tree pressed against the mausoleum's door. I was alive, barely breathing. I had suffered a stroke.

They took me to the hospital and treated me. I survived but was left paralyzed. I can't speak.

Looking in my pockets for means of identification, they found a wad of wet papers with ink smeared all over the pages. They threw the papers away.

I am thus in sole possession of the music I stole. I play it over and over in my mind, both in awe of its beauty and in despair at the heavy cost I incurred for retrieving it.

BIRTH OF A NEW SPECIES

When in doubt, blame the dark elves.
- Kevin Hearne

Modifications will add to the beautiful and harmonious diversity of nature.
- Charles Darwin, *The Origin of the Species*, Chapter 5

1

"The important thing," said Dolniss once again, "is to drain all the blood from a human's corpse before consuming it. I favor making three cuts, one across the neck, another below the groin, and the third down the chest, by the heart."

"*Ay*, love," mocked Ellvar. "You're getting pedantic in your old age. *Everyone* knows that." The young elf pouted at his lover derisively.

Dolniss tried not to let his irritation show. "It's a lesson that must not be forgotten. Human blood is rich in iron and salt. Both substances are harmful, and potentially lethal, to us elves. Drained human flesh is nutritious and tastes good. The choice is clear."

Ellvar felt argumentative that evening. "It's old-fashioned folks like you that keep us from making progress. Who can deny that a little blood enhances the flavor? I've tasted human blood more than once and it has done me no harm."

"Don't confuse luck with wisdom," replied the older elf.

He stopped honing the edge of his sword and came forward, placing a caressing hand on his young ward's shoulder. "There are only a few of us left to continue waging the war. Can't risk losing anyone to poor eating habits."

Ellvar shook his shoulder free and snorted. "Don't blame the state of the war on us, the new generation. We've been begging forever for a change in tactics. You insist on trying to lure humans into our underground caverns so we can ambush them. That strategy might have worked fine at some point in the past, but now humans don't fall for it anymore. They aren't as stupid as you seem to be."

That was one snide remark too many for Dolniss. He turned his back on the insolent whelp and moved his weapon honing to another hall.

2

Dolniss was loath to acknowledge that his lover had a point. The dark elves had been fighting the creatures of the surface, mainly the humans and the light-skinned elves known as the Ljósálfar, for many, many cycles of the moon. The surface dwellers had an advantage: they could move freely during the day, without being impaired by the sun's cruel rays. On the other hand, both humans and elves lacked night vision, and the humans' senses of hearing and smell were poor. Humans also fell easily into traps, were vulnerable to magic, and had little endurance in comparison with the elven races. It was amazing how they managed to survive despite their handicaps.

"The humans rule the skin of the world, but the rest of the world's body is ours," was an ancient boast of the Dökkálfar, as the dark elves were called by friend and foe alike. That boast had been meaningful once, but now the balance of power had shifted. Instead of penetrating the dark elves' domains and risking extermination, humans now saturated the entrances to the underworld with firebombs and depth charges, and sometimes tried to block the elves' "rabbit holes" and trap them beneath the surface. The hated

Ljósálfar also made periodic forays against their erstwhile relatives, causing great losses of life every time they launched such an attack.

Mother Arvees, the High Queen of the Dökkálfar, had been briefed on the changing face of the conflict, but she was many hundred seasons old and was set in her ways. "I'll send no fighting units above ground to have them slaughtered. Give me some other alternative and I'll consider it." She would not be moved easily, and the precarious status quo was maintained, to the disadvantage of the Dökkálfar.

3

As often happens, the war between humans and dark elves had started by accident. A millennium or two ago, a band of primitive humans exploring the edges of the North Continent had discovered a cove to which streams of sea creatures were attracted. The humans started bringing their fishing vessels to the cove and setting nets that would trap the abundant fish. Unbeknownst to the humans, however, the cove was a sacred spot for the dark elves, who emerged to the surface on cold evenings to chant their prayers to the moon and conduct arcane rites that ended in mass bacchanalia.

So, it came to pass one night that the fishing and the carousing coincided and interfered with each other, leading to a clash. The humans flung harpoons at the strange, otherworldly creatures that responded with eerie wailings as they were wounded. The elves retaliated by gathering beneath the humans' vessels and causing them to overturn. All but a couple of the humans perished; the survivors managed to swim back to safety and alerted their brethren. Skirmishes between the two species ensued, ultimately growing into organized warfare.

It was on that fateful night, long since forgotten, that the dark elves tried human flesh for the first time. They had captured an injured man and dragged him to the cove, where they began torturing him by slicing off portions of his body with knives, ripping gobs of bloody flesh, and tasting them. They found the still-warm meat flavorful, though the blood had a disagreeable metallic taste. Sampling the flesh of other humans, either dead or still alive, confirmed that killing man was not only a necessary activity in wartime but also a nourishing pastime, and human flesh became a sought-after delicacy.

Opinions were divided on whether the flesh of a still living prisoner was tastier than that of a corpse. Dolniss was among those who felt that, while some enjoyment was derived from witnessing the terror and pain of a human whose flesh was being cut off to be eaten before his eyes, the harrowing experience prompted the release of chemicals in the body of the victim that impaired the taste of the morsels. This controversy was never settled.

4

Another dispute that would not lend itself to easy resolution was the growing feud between Dolniss and Ellvar. They continued to have sex and enjoy each other physically, but copulation (whether homo- or heterosexual) was not regarded as an important activity by most dark elves. They enjoyed sex the same way they took pleasure in games of skill or chance: fine while it lasted, but not worthy of thinking much about it afterward. Dolniss was exceptional in that regard, for his attraction to Ellvar's body was coupled with an unconfessed affection that was rare among the self-centered Dökkálfar.

On the other hand, the daily sessions in which Dolniss tried to impart the wisdom of the ancients on Ellvar became increasingly tense. Ellvar was always antagonistic and challenged every point of dogma propounded by Dolniss—even the universal belief that the Dökkálfar and the Ljósálfar were once a single people. "No way that can be true," argued Ellvar. "Those light-adoring snobs are more like humans, not at all like us. They are merciless killers that have responded to our requests for peace with violence. They have never liked us, as much as we abhor them."

While their opposing views were raised in the context of abstract issues, it became abundantly clear that Ellvar was no longer interested in learning from his lover and master or even dealing that much with him. Respect and affection, when they exist, are fleeting emotions among the Dökkálfar. They seldom rise and can be easily throttled.

Given their gradual drifting apart, it came as no surprise when one night toward the end of the cold season Ellvar came to Dolniss's quarters and announced matter-of-factly, "I've come to say goodbye. I'm leaving the depressing caverns that the Dökkálfar call home and moving up to the surface."

Dolniss received the news with astonishment and more than a bit of sorrow. "Have you lost your mind? How are you going to survive? The surface lands are full of deadly traps for us Dökkálfar. Not a cycle of the moon will pass before you are slain by humans or dwarves, or enslaved by the Ljósálfar!"

Ellvar brushed aside his mentor's objections. "I haven't been idle. I've been looking for ways to make it up there... And I've found them."

"What are those ways?"

Ellvar gave a mysterious wave of the arms. "I'm not telling you. Suffice it to say that they involve magic. Through them, humans will provide nourishment for me and my kin, without having to engage them in battle. I'll continue to hide by day and hunt by night, but my ways will be safer, for they are the ones I have invented."

Dolniss realized that it would be fruitless to attempt to dissuade his former ward from whatever erratic course of action he was planning. For a moment, he considered restraining Ellvar by force, but while physical violence by a mature dark elf upon a younger one was permitted, it could be exerted only in cases of societal need. The current situation posed no threat to anyone but Ellvar himself, so it did not qualify. He bit his lip to restrain tears from flowing, gave the young elf a last embrace, and let him go.

5

Ellvar was gone for a long time; so long, that many in his own House had forgotten his existence. His reappearance in the main Cavern was greeted with shock by even the few who remembered him, for he appeared to have undergone a profound change.

The most visible manifestations of his transformation were physical. He had grown very tall, such that he was about the size of an average adult human, and his body had become wiry and muscular. His dark gray skin exhibited a reddish undertone and his hair, formerly white, was now silvery and flowed in rivulets down the small of his back. But the greatest change was displayed in his eyes: once pale, they had turned scarlet and were matched by crimson gums that contrasted with razor-sharp, gleaming teeth.

But beyond the physical signs, Ellvar's new persona was evidenced by the self-assurance of his stance, the arrogance of his movements, and a palpable malevolence that radiated from him like a dark cloud that enveloped the space his body occupied.

He did not come alone. He was escorted by two fierce-looking female Dökkálfar and a gaggle of young elves of all ages. In all, it was an imposing, fear-inducing knot of dark elves, in comparison with which the rest of the elves seemed weak and small.

Dolniss had been at work on his shop but was drawn outside by the hubbub of voices in the plaza. Ellvar, who appeared headed for the lofty palace of the Mother, did a double take upon recognizing his former master and changed course to meet him.

"Hail, Master!" he greeted, in a tone that was all but respectful.

"Welcome, Ellvar," replied Dolniss soberly, restraining his emotions the best he could. And then, "You seem to be in good health."

Ellvar could not wait to gloat. "Yes, Master. Despite your dire warnings, I've survived on the surface, and even prospered." He ran a large, gloved hand over his chest.

Dolniss would not rise to the bait, and instead of inquiring further about Ellvar's adventures he replied, nodding in the direction of the Mother's palace, "Arvees will be glad to see one of her lost children return to the fold."

"Yes, I've come to see her, but don't intend to grovel or, as you call it, return to the fold. I'm here to seek recognition."

Dolniss could not refrain from asking, "Recognition for what?"

"I've created a new kind of elf, which I demand be counted along with the races of the higher beings such as the Dökkálfar, the Ljósálfar, the humans, and the dwarves. I'm starting down here, for I hope my fellow dark elves will be the first to acknowledge and admire my accomplishment."

Now drawn in, Dolniss asked, "What sort of new elf is that?"

"I don't have a name for it yet. Let me describe what I have done and perhaps you'll help me name the new species." He stopped to gather his thoughts and then continued.

"You were right in warning me about the dangers posed by the humans and the Ljósálfar. I never could figure out how to protect myself from the Ljósálfar, other than avoid engaging them in combat in which I could easily be killed. For that reason, ever since I ascended to the surface, I have made it my practice to hide during the day and emerge only at night, when the Ljósálfar are dormant.

"Humans are less of a problem, because among other things they are vulnerable to magic. I'm not a practitioner of the Higher Arts, but like every elf, I've learned the basic spells that may help me survive an encounter with an enemy. One simple spell that I can cast upon a human is the *abasement of the will* spell, which forces its victims to yield to the suggestions or orders of the spellcaster. Of course, every Dökkálfar older than an infant knows how to resist such a spell and render its commands mere suggestions that can be safely ignored. For humans, though, the *abasement of the will* spell can, in many instances, force a human—particularly a young or weak one—to submit to most demands made upon him under the spell.

"A discussion we had many moons ago about the savoring of human blood and its potential consequences stayed in my mind as I began considering the possibility of leaving the Underworld. I had continued ingesting human blood in ever-increasing quantities and had succeeded in mastering its ill effects. My kidneys had become capable of disposing of iron particles with only a slight irritation upon evacuating. By the time I was ready to say my goodbyes here, I was essentially immune to the adverse effects of human blood on my system.

"Then inspiration hit me. If I could, by means of the *abasement of the will* spell, induce a human opponent to allow me to drink his blood, I could get nourishment without combat risks and could incapacitate, and ultimately slay, my opponent. I dared not try the spell to suggest more drastic actions by the human, such as killing himself or offering his body as a sacrifice, because the self-preservation instinct that every living being has would thwart my efforts and put me at risk of discovery. But letting me partake of some of his blood was not felt to be a deadly threat. Of course, by repeating the process I could ultimately weaken my victim enough to cause him to die or become vulnerable to a physical attack.

"When I went up to the surface, I hid near a settlement of humans. I started appearing in their quarters at night, seeking in the darkness for suitable victims upon whom to experiment. I soon discovered that the very young, the very old, and the weakest females were the best targets. I tried my hand with growing youth and even older men but generally failed. I'm still working on that problem and have every confidence that I'll succeed soon.

"So, the long and the short of it is that I have created a

new type of creature, of which I, my wives, and my children are the first specimens. We are the *improved* Dökkálfar, creatures of the night that live off the blood of humans. We are on our way to finally overcoming one of our most hated enemies. What do you think of that?"

Dolniss remained silent for a long while. At length, shaking his head, he replied, "What you have done is wondrous but foul. You have transformed the noble race of the Dökkálfar into vile leeches, cowards who don't overcome their enemies through strength and cunning but by using loathsome stratagems. I'm sure there will be some among us that will applaud you, but I predict that the majority of the Dökkálfar will reject you and the new kind of being you represent."

"I regret that you feel that way, but no matter," replied Ellvar, turning his back without more on his former friend.

6

Dolniss's prediction proved accurate. There was passionate debate among the Dökkálfar, in which not only the nobles but the clerics, the foot soldiers, and even the commoners took part. The vast majority of the dark elves rejected Ellvar's implicit proposal that they all become blood-sucking fiends and thus change the time-honored ways of the Dökkálfar. A few, however, sided with him and demanded that the dark elves move to the surface and, under Ellvar's leadership, vanquish the humans once and for all.

Matters degenerated into violent encounters between the two groups. Finally, Mother Arvees intervened and decreed that there be a trial by combat to resolve the controversy. The two sides chose their champions. Ellvar's supporters nominated him; his opponents had trouble finding one willing to oppose the imposing youth in combat until Dolniss volunteered, for he was willing to risk his life to put an end to the madness.

They clashed at midnight in the plaza by Mother Arvees's palace. Elves were gathered all over the area, standing in the porticos of palaces, staring out of windows, even hanging atop the stalagmites that dotted the cavern's rocky floor.

The combatants entered from opposite ends of the plaza. It was evident at a glance there was a great disparity between them. Dolniss was a nobleman and a trained cleric; his armor was of shining *mithril*, light and flexible so his movements would not be impeded. Ellvar was wearing adamantine armor, which offered less protection and was heavier. The same could be said about their weapons of choice. Dolniss, an expert warrior, carried the two *mithril* swords, whose coordinated use required much talent and practice. Ellvar had a single sword, which he supplemented with a variety of auxiliary weapons, including a whip of fangs, a short lance, and a spinneret. Attached to his back was a sack with light pellets and other distracting devices.

The fighters approached each other gingerly, each measuring the other up and trying to anticipate his attack. Ellvar struck first, casting a blow at Dolniss's chest and retreating quickly, counting on his natural agility to avoid Dolniss's riposte. Dolniss parried the blow and advanced, brandishing both swords simultaneously and drawing intricate patterns in the air that changed too fast for the eye to catch.

From that point on, the fight proceeded predictably. Ellvar was overmatched, and only his agility saved him from receiving a fatal wound. He tried each of the auxiliary weapons on Dolniss, who severed the whip with a single thrust of one of the swords, forced the lance out of Ellvar's hand with a series of well-directed blows, and ignored the light pellets that Ellvar cast at him.

Ten minutes into the fight, Ellvar was tired from the continuous chase by Dolniss, and his movements had become slower and less coordinated. Dolniss, who continued to press inexorably at his opponent, finally uttered an angry cry and wrestled Ellvar's sword from his hand with a devastating blow from both his weapons. He pushed the defenseless Ellvar down to the ground and readied to deliver a death blow.

"Please kiss me one last time. I want to die with your

taste on my lips," pleaded Ellvar to his enemy, who stood menacingly above him.

Dolniss hesitated but then, remembering the times when they had tangled in a joyful embrace, bent over his former ward to reach his lips. Quick as a viper, Ellvar angled up his head, sunk his sharp teeth into his lover's neck, and bit with a ferocity driven by malice and despair. Before Dolniss had time to react, a wide gash had opened below his chin, and a stream of red blood was issuing from the wound. Ellvar started slurping it greedily, smacking his lips as he swallowed.

Pandemonium erupted in the plaza. Cries of anger, shock, and disgust resonated, and half the spectators rose to their feet, shaking their fists. In her presiding box, Arvees issued a sharp cry and motioned her guards down to the floor of the plaza, where they seized Ellvar, blood still dripping from his half-open mouth. Behind him, Dolniss was convulsing one last time, as life escaped through a severed carotid artery.

Ellvar was brought before the livid Mother. "You have committed an unforgivable crime! Do you have anything to say in your defense?"

Ellvar remained silent, a self-satisfied expression on his face.

"I can have you executed for killing one of the senior members of my staff" she started.

"No, my lady, you can't. It was a trial by combat, and death of a participant is a permissible outcome."

"Still, I have the power to order your death. But you have caused enough grief to our people already, and your death could bring about worse things. But this I will do. I order that you, your family, and anyone who supports your cause be banished forever from the Underworld. Return to the surface and lead your depraved life whichever way you choose. But pray your path doesn't intersect with that of the Dökkálfar people. You are no longer one of us, and we disown you!"

Ellvar bowed his head so that the Mother would not see

the surge of regret that suddenly drowned him. He turned around quickly and headed for his quarters, anxious to depart.

The new species would come into its own without help from others.

Showdown in the Panhandle

"If I owned Texas and Hell, I would rent out Texas and live in Hell."
- General Philip Henry Sheridan

In the spring of 1890, Harry Gunnach was forcibly booted out of the Nicolett Hotel in Lubbock for cheating at card games. He was accused of having some way of figuring out other players' hands and using his skill to swindle hundreds of dollars from the merchants and cattle ranchers of the town.

Soon, a mob of dispossessed gamblers assembled and began chasing after Harry, seeking to recover the monies he had stolen. He ran for his life and barely escaped his pursuers by purloining a pony from a stable on the outskirts of town. After a three-day forced march, Harry covered the hundred miles between Lubbock and the new town of Oneida (which was later to become Amarillo) and made a stop.

Oneida's original location had been in a low-lying area prone to flooding and, after the disastrous 1889 rainy season, had just been moved to higher ground. The move had led to an influx of merchants, cattle buyers, and settlers, whose business had spurred the opening of the 66 Saloon next to the Crescent Hotel. Harry had heard about the 66 from another card sharp in Lubbock, who claimed it was already the roughest new bar in Texas and the easiest place to get killed outside of Mason County. Harry had been intrigued by the implicit challenge in the description; its memory drew him to gallop toward Oneida as the citizens of Lubbock organized a posse to lynch him.

Harry hated the West. He was originally from Philadelphia, but had learned early in life that the City of Brotherly Love had no affection for him. After leaving Philadelphia, he had been forced to relocate scores of times, moving from one Eastern town to another in search of places where he could pass unnoticed. The vast emptiness of Texas had lured him in, but soon the big cities like Houston and San Antonio had become inhospitable. He continued to search for a place where he could thrive in obscurity as a card sharp, and at last discovered the northern corner of the state and chose it as the area most likely to fit his needs.

He had several hundred dollars left from his last games in Lubbock. He got himself a room at the Crescent and paid a visit to the town barber for a haircut and a shave. Then, dressed in his business suit, he walked the few steps over to the 66, which was a crude wooden shack squat on the yellow dirt of the panhandle. He entered the saloon at sunset and sat at a side table, ordered a whiskey, and nursed his drink, waiting for a card game to get going.

It did not take long. Six men had already gathered around the long table next to the bar; two seats remained empty. Harry watched for a few minutes, concentrating on the emotional and physical signatures emitted by the players. He concluded that four of them were amateurs, cattle ranch hands come to gamble away their pay. Another player, a giant of a bearded man named Karl, seemed to be an experienced player, for he took few risks and displayed no feelings on his stolid face. The sixth player was another big fellow called Lucius, who said little and sprouted a white goatee on his square jaw. Lucius' emotions seemed shrouded by a veil that Harry's probing could not penetrate. Harry concluded that the man was some sort of a card sharp, like himself.

They were playing Five Card Draw, a version of poker that had become increasingly popular since the War Between the States. Harry liked that variation of the game, since each player immediately saw the hand he was dealt and couldn't stop broadcasting his feelings about it. For someone like Harry, able to read other people's emotions, no bluffs could disguise weak holdings. He did not need to know the exact nature of the hand held by each player to be aware of who held losers and which had good prospects, although that information would become more evident as the betting progressed.

There was a break as the players got their liquor refills and two of them went outside to relieve themselves. Harry sidled over to the gamblers' table and asked whether he could join the game in progress. Karl, the man whom Harry pegged as the experienced player, seemed to be in charge of the game and nodded his assent as Harry took one of the empty chairs, two seats to the left of him.

The players' reactions to the hands they were dealt by Lucius were revelatory. After nickel antes were deposited, each player received five cards, one at a time, all face down. The remainder of the deck was placed aside, secured under Lucius' half-empty whiskey glass. The players picked up their cards and held them in their hands, being careful to keep them concealed.

Harry closed his eyes and cast his mind around the table. Two of the amateur players were unhappy with their hands. One inadvertently sighed in resignation; the fourth's mood had become upbeat. Karl only registered a subtle feeling of disquiet. Lucius's mind was blank.

A first round of betting began. One of the ranch hands immediately dropped out. The rest, starting with the one to the left of Lucius, placed bets that either raised or met the existing high bet. By the end of the round, another of the ranch hands had dropped out.

Each of the remaining players then specified how many of the cards in his hand he wanted replaced and received fresh cards from the deck in place of the ones discarded. There was more for Harry to learn then: one of the ranch hands asked for two cards, though he seemed unhappy with what he held previously and remained so after he was dealt replacement cards. Harry concluded he was getting ready to bluff. The other, who had previously seemed in a good mood, remained somewhat upbeat, though no more so than before the cards he had discarded were replaced with fresh ones. Harry knew he held at most a two pair. Karl had asked for two cards and had registered just a smidgen of satisfaction with the new hand he had gotten. Lucius drew only one card for himself and remained aloof after the exchange. Harry had asked for three cards and had given only a casual glance at them. He did not expect to win this hand.

There was a second round of betting, after which Harry could predict the personalities and likely behaviors of most of the players for the rest of the night. Three of the cattle ranch hands were transparent: they would immediately telegraph the quality of their cards. The other one would try to bluff and pretend his hand was better than it actually was. Karl proved hard to read, except if he held a very good or very poor hand. Lucius remained a mystery.

Play continued for over two hours, through over a dozen games. At the end, all four cattle ranch hands had lost everything and had gone home or remained around the table as spectators. Karl was losing moderately. Lucius was ahead by about twenty dollars. Harry had won about forty.

Karl then proposed: "Let this be the last round. I'm getting tired and have a lot of work ahead of me tomorrow." Harry and Lucius agreed.

Lucius then suggested: "How about a twenty-dollar ante for the last game?" They all agreed. Karl opened the bidding with a five-dollar bet. Harry raised ten; Lucius and Karl checked.

Karl asked for a three-card replacement. After seeing his new cards, his eyes gleamed for just one second on the otherwise stony face. Harry sensed that Karl's pulse had quickened. Lucius discarded one card, but again, Harry could not detect any emotions. Harry asked for three cards, and a quick look at his new hand showed a full house, sevens and queens.

Now the second round of betting started. Karl bet

twenty, and Harry raised twenty on him. Lucius folded. Karl then raised two hundred, and Harry glanced at him briefly. The hopeful gleam in Karl's eye was there, but then dimmed; at the end, his pulse had quickened and his heart was beating a bit faster. Harry realized he was bluffing. He felt like raising again, but it was not wise to be too greedy on his first night out; there would be more money to be made tomorrow. He called Karl's bet, and they went into the showdown. Karl only had three kings. Harry's full house won, and he readied to take the pot.

"Not so fast," growled Karl. "You've been cheating. You are a damn card sharp!"

"Why do you say that?" replied Harry. "What have I done?"

"Somehow you knew my hand," countered Karl. "I initially had a couple of kings, but when I drew the three cards, I saw another king and momentarily mistook a jack for a king, so I thought I had four kings. Then I raised two hundred and stared at the cards again. I immediately saw my error, but nothing could be done about it. Normally I would have expected you to hesitate for a moment or two, wondering what to do. You didn't, but jumped on my bid right away. And your hand was good, but not good enough to be so confident. Somehow you knew I had goofed."

"That's hogwash," said Harry, getting to his feet.

"Cheater!" screamed Karl, getting up himself, seizing Harry by the waist and forcibly throwing him on the table, scattering cards, money, and glasses in the process.

"Let me go!" demanded Harry, but he was a small man and no match for the irate Karl.

Lucius, who had remained silent since dropping out of the game, cleared his throat. "I spent years in Japan training in *mushin no shin*, a form of mind control. From my training, I can play cards automatically, letting my brain simply plow through, while still well conscious of my surroundings. I noticed the same thing Karl said, but saw no signs of card sharping as such. I reckon this man won the games fair and square."

Karl let go of Harry and turned his rage onto Lucius. "What makes you such an expert on cheating? Are you in cahoots with this bastard?"

"No, sir," replied Lucius icily. "I am a marshal sent from Austin by the Governor to investigate the spate of recent killings in this town. Right now, I'm going to take this man into custody for questioning. Please step aside." He got up and took Harry by the arm and led him out of the saloon.

"Now, you better come clean. What's your real game?" Lucius demanded of Harry in a tone that left no room for prevarication.

"I do have a special gift," answered Harry. "Somehow, I'm able to tune into the emotions of others around me. With time and practice, I have learned to profit from this talent. But there is nothing criminal about my gift. A good listener is almost as talented as I am, as my father used to say." Harry shuddered apologetically.

"Come on, there has to be more to your story. You're a Cryptid, aren't you?"

Harry gave a deep sigh. "How did you know?"

"Back in Austin, Cryptids are getting to be common despite the city's efforts to get rid of them. You can tell them apart because they are sort of scrawny and pale, like you are. But their main giveaway is their necks, because the glands around their necks are swollen up and they try to cover them by wearing scarves or bandanas, the way you do. Those glands send something into the air that helps them figure out what decent folks are thinking so they can take advantage. That's how they beat regular folks at card games, and cheat them in business and get rich at their expense."

Harry reacted violently to the accusation. "I'm no damned Cryptid like Bigfoot or the Goatman and the monsters of popular legends. I'm only a regular man trying to make a living the best way I know how."

"That's not the whole story, is it? You better come clean, or I'm arresting you." He seized Harry by the arm and started to pull him away.

Harry pressed his lips tightly, as if he were unwilling to say more, but at the end relented. "Word among us is that our breed comes from the backcountry in Appalachia, where a knot of Scottish families had settled. There was a lot of inbreeding, and soon newborns started to show what we call empathy. At first, we didn't think much of it other than it was nice that our kids didn't get into fights because they understood each other so well. But then, sometime in the 1750s, we were driven out of our lands by the government and forced to spread into the towns and cities of the South.

"Once our peculiarity started to be noticed we became outcasts. Not only were we visibly different from the general population, but we had a perceived advantage over the rest of the people. Our kids were resented because they did better academically, so in some towns they were barred from schools and had to be taught at home by their relatives. As we grew more numerous, our people worked hard and succeeded in all areas where human interaction is a factor. We are good teachers, doctors, lawyers and judges, preachers, merchants and salesmen, politicians, and even card players like me.

"But that success has come at a heavy cost. We live in fear and have to hide what we are, because if we are recognized, we are fired from our jobs, roughed up, arrested without cause, expelled from some towns, and imprisoned. There have been a number of unprovoked riots resulting in some of our people being put to death.

"So, yes, I have chosen to make a living playing cards. I'm pretty good at it, and the stupidity of my opponents allows me to win most of the time and cut my losses when the cards turn against me. Arrest me if you will, but I do nothing that any ordinary citizen wouldn't do if he could."

Lucius let go of Harry's arm. "All of what you say may be true, but it doesn't excuse you. You and your kind may think you are victims, but you still use your gift, if that's what it is, for your benefit at the expense of normal folks. If I were not here on a law enforcement mission, I would be tempted to put a bullet through your skull, but I don't want to add another dead scoundrel to this town's tally." After a moment of reflection, he added: "I reckon it'll be enough to run you out of Oneida, but the word will get around these parts, so you might as well get out of the state. Go to the Territories to ply your trade. Maybe you'll have better luck with them rubes in New Mexico or Oklahoma than here. And maybe you should change your line of business. Remember the '84 election? That preacher George Ball who almost cost Grover Cleveland the presidency was a Cryptid like you.

"Do whatever you like, but don't come back to Texas or I'll put you away!"

Harry went back to the Crescent and climbed on his horse, tired but eager to skip town. He was last seen galloping away in a cloud of dust.

Later that day, three men from the Lubbock posse arrived in Oneida, looking for Harry and the money he had stolen. They left after an hour, chasing after a fugitive they would never catch: Harry had crossed into New Mexico.

Harry settled in the Taos area, changed his name to Gunn, and became an influential local politician during the Rio Hondo gold fever period. He discovered, as other Cryptids had, that more money can be made in public life than in saloon card games, with much less risk of getting shot.

LIEBESTOD

Zu spät! Trotziger Mann! Strafst du mich
so mit härtestem Bann?
Ganz ohne Huld meiner Leidens-Schuld?
Nicht meine Klagen darf ich dir sagen?
Nur einmal, ach! nur einmal noch! -
Tristan! - Ha! - horch! Er wacht!Geliebter!
- Wagner, Tristan und Isolde, *Act 3*

1.

The day of her sixteenth birthday found Talia feeling despondent, as her life was slipping away without accomplishments. As she readied to blow the candles on the cake, her mother encouraged, "Make a wish, dear. I have the feeling it will come true."

Talia shot back, perhaps a little harshly, "You know what I wish. I have said it a million times. I want to be an opera singer. But that's never going to happen."

Her mother gave a tired smile. "Yes, we've heard it often enough. When you were only a six-year-old pipsqueak, you heard someone on the radio doing the Bell Song from *Lakmé* and were hooked."

"I'm sorry, Mom. I didn't mean to snap. You and Dad have done all you could to help me with my dream. You enrolled me in a school for children interested in the arts. You paid for my acting and language lessons. You found me a voice tutor, who trained me. Now I've reached a dead end. All of that seems to have been for nothing."

As everyone retired for the night, Talia snatched a bottle of apricot schnapps and absconded with it to her bedroom, intending to get drunk. She did not like the apricot brandy, but she soldiered on, filling one shot glass, downing it in one or two gulps, and refilling it.

Before long half of the bottle was gone, Talia's head was spinning and her grip on the glass was loosening. "One more shot," she said as she poured another measure into the glass. She never finished it; the glass and the bottle dropped on the carpet, and she fell backward onto her bed and passed out.

Her stupor was not peaceful. Confused images kept drifting in and out of focus before her eyes. One figure kept coming back to her, each time more vividly: an odd woman, veiled, all dressed in black. Talia finally realized that a lady was there, disapproval showing on her wrinkled features.

"Who are you?" queried Talia.

The response was puzzling. "Some call me The Queen of Spades. I am your secret godmother."

"I didn't know I had a godmother," said Talia dreamily.

"I said it was secret. Your mother and I have had dealings for years, and she asked me to come to you on your special day."

"What do you want from me?"

"Why, I have come to give you a present, since you became of age today. Are you ready for your gift?"

"What's it?" The old lady was not holding any parcels.

"It is the gift you have been craving for: a career as an opera singer, if you want it."

"It would be a great gift, but nobody can give it to me," replied Talia, disconsolate.

"I can," said the Queen of Spades. "But before I do, I must be sure that this is what you truly want. Did I hear you say that your life is to sing, and singing is your life?"

"Yes."

"Are you certain you want your life to be like that? Such

a gift cannot be returned and comes with a price."

"Yes, that's what I want," replied Talia without hesitation. "But what's the price?"

"Your life will be ruled by the gift."

"Well, that's a price I'm willing to pay."

"Then it shall be as you desire. Go to sleep. In the morning, call the office at the Juilliard School and inquire whether there are any scholarships available for which you can apply. The answer will be yes. If you apply, you will be admitted."

"I don't believe you."

"Just give it a try. And now, try to sleep off that disgusting inebriation." Without more, there was a swish of fabric, and the old lady was gone.

2.

The following morning Talia was terribly sorry about her drinking bout. It was not until early afternoon that she remembered being visited by the Queen of Spades and receiving her birthday gift. She smiled ruefully at being so stupid as to get drunk on apricot brandy and dream up such garbage. Later in the afternoon, however, she decided to call Juilliard. What did she have to lose?

When she was connected to the admissions office, she was told that yes, due to unexpected resignations, there were openings in the Marcus Institute for Vocal Arts. Registration was already closed for the academic year, but because of the vacancies, they would consider new applications. Talia begged to be sent an application immediately. The admissions officer agreed to forward the forms to Talia by overnight mail.

That was the start of what turned out to be a remarkable three-year course of study at Juilliard, which led to a graduation with honors and a successful audition at the Metropolitan Opera House, where she was hired to become a member of the chorus until an opportunity as a soloist became available.

A year later, Talia was home cooking dinner when her phone rang. She was dumbfounded when the suave voice on the line identified its owner as the Met's principal conductor, who, she had met during her successful audition. After greetings, he asked, "Tell me, *cara* Talia, do you by any chance know the role of Rosina, besides the aria that you sang so well at the audition and won you a place with us?"

"Yes, maestro, I studied the role because my voice coach said it fitted my voice well."

"How would you like to sing *Barber* at the Met?"

"Well, that would be wonderful. When would it be?"

"How about tonight?"

"Why me? I am only a singer with the chorus, barely a year off graduating from Juilliard."

"The soprano who is to sing Rosina in the Met's new production of *The Barber of Seville* was injured in a car crash this afternoon. The Met is caught in a bind because the understudy for the part of Rosina has quit after an argument with the stage manager and is on her way to the West Coast. Many substitute singers are potentially available, but none can come on a few hours' notice. They were about to cancel the premiere of the show when I had an idea: bringing in, just for that night, the young singer who had provided that stunning rendition of Rosina's aria, *Una Voce Poco Fa*. That's you."

A long silence ensued. Talia hesitated. "I never performed the part onstage and wouldn't know what to do."

"The other singers will help you out. Plus, you are supposed to be an ingénue, and acting a bit clumsy would not be out of character."

"I may not remember my lines."

"Just give a quick read to the score. We have the best prompters in the business."

"But, sir, this is a monumental gamble for me."

"I know, but I have a hunch that it will all work out

well."

"Okay," she sighed. "I'll do it. Wish me luck."

"Be at the Met no later than seven so you can get fitted for a dress, made up, and meet your colleagues."

"I'll do it," she said again, trying to hide the tremor in her voice. "Thanks for all you have done for me."

"You are welcome. I'm doing it for the Met as well."

At seven o'clock, Talia emerged from a taxi, score of *Barber* under an arm and a ratty coat on the other. She was greeted at the opera house by what seemed like the entire company. At ten minutes to eight, the conductor came into the dressing room as Talia was donning one of the gowns she would wear that evening. "Are you ready, my dear?" he asked breezily.

"I'm scared stiff, but am as ready as I will ever be," she assured him.

* * *

The conductor entered the pit and bowed. Before the applause had died out, he turned to the orchestra and launched into the overture to *Barber*. Seven minutes later, the curtain was raised.

Soon it was Talia's turn to make her appearance. There was an expectant silence as the doors to the balcony opened and Talia, radiant in a silk nightgown, came forward. Her initial lines were short and unremarkable; the action then moved to the mansion's living room, where Talia burst into *Una Voce Poco Fa*. If anything, her performance that night was even more brilliant than in her audition; at the end, she uttered very loudly a sustained high C and made a graceful pirouette as the music died down.

A stunned silence followed, and then all dikes burst, and an ovation the likes of which was seldom heard at the Met resounded.

3.

The Met offered Talia a contract to perform in *Barber* for the rest of its run, alternating with a recovering Madame Dimitrova. People flocked to hear her the few days where she had the lead, and she did not disappoint her growing fan base. The success of that season was crowned when a European label offered her a contract for her first solo album.

Her professional happiness, however, was not matched by harmony at home. After being hired by the Met to be a member of the chorus, Talia had met Sergio, a handsome Argentinian tenor who was also with the chorus. Their friendship blossomed into romance and one night he proposed, and they were engaged. Marriage followed and Talia and Sergio moved to a modest apartment in Brooklyn.

Sergio became resentful of Talia's overnight success and began looking elsewhere for entertainment. One night, Talia returned home unexpectedly because her flight had been canceled, only to find Sergio curled up with a pretty blonde.

After a bitter divorce, Talia was free again, reflecting that she was not better off than the Rosina of the *Barber* for, like Rosina's husband, hers had also shown himself to be a lecher.

4.

Talia's voice eventually matured, and she began taking on dramatic soprano roles. She also met and fell in love with Armand D'Escoubet, a French journalist who was a foreign correspondent for a news agency. They married and settled for a domestic life in which both traveled frequently and only saw each other when their schedules permitted.

The San Francisco Opera decided to mount a new production of Wagner's Ring cycle, and invited her to sing the part of Sieglinde, the tragic lover of her brother Siegmund, in *Die Walküre*. Staging a new Ring cycle is a complex affair, and the preparations for all four operas extended for almost two years. At the end, the production was ready, and Talia was scheduled to appear in the second opera of the cycle when it opened the following spring.

As the premiere of the Ring approached, Armand was detailed to Africa to report on hostilities between warring factions in South Sudan, so he was going to miss this important musical event. "Fear not" consoled Talia, "we have a contract for the video of the entire cycle. I'll give you a copy of *Walküre* so you can see your wifey in action."

She had a dream the eve of the opening of *Walküre*. An old woman in black was sitting in one of the boxes at the Opera House watching her perform. Then, the lady was in her dressing room, offering her a large square box wrapped in gold leaf paper with a scarlet bow encircling it. It was beautiful but had a sinister aura.

"It is a present to celebrate your accomplishments."

"Can I open it?"

"Of course," replied the old woman with an enigmatic smile.

Talia tore the wrapping to reveal a black wooden box. She lifted the lid, only to find that the box was empty, yet did not feel empty. A cold draft emanated from the box and a wet smell, like that of turned earth, filled her nostrils. "What is this?" she asked, bewildered.

"You will know when the show is over."

With that, Talia awoke, feeling an unease that stayed with her through the day.

After the performance of *Walküre*, Talia returned to her apartment and went to bed almost at once. She was asleep when the telephone rang. She could barely discern the voice, heavily accented, that once she acknowledged her identity, stated, "Madame, I'm with the United Nations Peacekeeping Force in Juba, South Sudan." There was a pause and when Talia was getting ready to say something, the voice continued. "I'm afraid I have bad news."

Talia clawed at her pillow. "There was an attack by a mercenary band on a U.N. outpost in the Jonglei region. The attackers launched incendiary bombs and burned the building to the ground. A number of people were inside, both U.N. peacekeepers and foreign reporters. Your husband was among them…"

"Oh, no!" screamed Talia. "Is he… all right?"

"I am sorry… No. Everyone perished in the fire."

Talia exercised the self-control her training had given her, and asked tightly, "Who do I need to speak to in order to have his remains flown here for burial?"

Again, there was a silence. Finally, the voice replied, "I'm sorry. The attackers used thermite, a substance that burns through even solid steel. Only cinders are left of the people who were in the building."

Talia realized that Armand was gone forever, and she did not even have the consolation of mourning him properly. Like Sieglinde in *Walküre*…

All of a sudden, she recalled the gift she had received and its terrible price, and shed bitter tears. She addressed her benefactor in desperation. "Wherever you are, I don't want your gift anymore. It has cost me all too much!" But her pleas remained unanswered.

5.

Talia resolved to leave the stage, but her passion for singing was too strong to give it up at once. Instead, she agreed to appear infrequently, only in comedies or dramas with happy endings. Her passion for the stage started to wane, and in the end, she took an early retirement.

One evening, her old friend the lead conductor of the Met—now an octogenarian approaching retirement himself—came to visit her and broached the subject of a new production with which he intended to close his career. Would she be interested in singing the leading role of Isolde in a forthcoming staging of *Tristan und Isolde*? The Met had succeeded in retaining the great Wolfgang Neiderhaus to sing the Tristan role. Would she please consider it?

Talia's initial reaction was to reject the idea, but then she remembered the immortal love duet in Act 2 of the opera and realized how empty her life had been since Armand's passing. What did she have left to live for? What else did she have to lose? She gritted her teeth as she assented. "I'll do Isolde for this run. But then I'll sing no more."

The night before the premiere Talia was having dinner at home with friends when the telephone rang. She almost did not pick up the receiver; she had the premonition that another dreadful call was about to change her life again. Ultimately, she answered, and a very American voice greeted her. "Ms. Suárez, please."

"Speaking," she replied.

"I'm Dr. Norman Weinberg calling from the Burn Center at New York Presbyterian."

Talia's heart skipped a beat. "How can I help you?"

"We have been treating a patient that was flown here from Paris. He asked us to contact you."

"What's his name?" shouted Talia.

"Armand D'Escoubet."

"That's impossible!" shrieked Talia. "He has been dead for years."

The voice replied, "Well, he is here and is near death. He wants to say goodbye to you."

"I'll be right there." Talia slammed down the receiver, grabbed a coat, and rushed out of the apartment.

At the hospital, she was ushered to a private room at the end of a hallway. A man, his body covered with tubes, IV drips, and other devices rested in bed. His features were all covered with sterile gauze, but his eyes were open, and his regard was anguished.

A doctor came into the room and led Talia to the corridor outside. "I am Dr. Weinberg. We spoke on the phone."

"How's he?" asked Talia, barely able to articulate her questions. "And how did he get here?"

"We don't know all the details," began the doctor, "but this is the information that was given to us by the hospital in Paris. Mr. D'Escoubet was the victim of an act of war in Africa. The house where he was staying was firebombed; luckily, he was outside smoking and escaped the death that visited the others. However, he was severely burned. He was driven by jeep to the nearest village and then transported to the capital, from where he was flown to Paris and taken to the Hôpital Cochin, the central burn treatment center of that city.

"His employer wanted to contact you, but he forbade it. He was burned beyond recognition and wanted to spare you the pain of seeing him in that condition. They reluctantly honored his wishes, and in the meantime, the staff at Cochin did a marvelous job keeping him alive.

"He lingered for the next three years, experiencing progressive multiple organ dysfunctions, but he has a strong constitution and was able to cling to life until a few days ago, when it became clear that he was soon to die. He then asked to be flown here and held until the end was at hand, at which time you were to be notified."

Talia went back into the room and gingerly took hold of her husband's hand. She could count the fragile bones as she pressed it close to her chest. No longer capable of holding back, she questioned him bitterly, "Why didn't you come into my arms when there was still time?"

There was no immediate response, but at length, he uttered hoarsely, "Talia, please forgive me. I've always loved you."

The effort was too great, and he collapsed on the bed.

A few minutes later, he expired.

6.

Friends took Talia back to her apartment, undressed her, and put her to bed. One of them started to call the Met to advise that Talia would not make it to the opening night, but she raised herself from the bed and cried: "*No!* I *must* be there. I *will* be there! I've paid too high a price…!"

The Talia that arrived at the opera house before the performance was pale, disheveled, her face puffed from crying and lack of sleep, her hair a wild tangle of graying curls. She would talk to nobody but allowed the staff to make her up and dress her.

She sleepwalked through the first act, and it was only in the love scene at the end of the second act that she came to life and responded wildly to Neiderhaus's ardent declarations. The tenor was taken aback by the desperate tinge in her voice but matched her cries with his controlled voice, passionate yet full of lyricism. When their love tryst was discovered and Tristan was gravely wounded, there was an audible gasp throughout the audience; people remained in their seats after the curtain fell, stunned.

During intermission, Talia went to her dressing room and collapsed. She could not bear the heaviness in her heart, as Armand's loss continued to sink in. She woke up to the sight of an old woman in black standing silently by her side.

"I told you I don't want your gift!" she shouted at the apparition. "It has given me nothing but grief! Please take it! Stop messing with my life and let me die in peace!"

The old woman shook her head. "I'm very sorry, child. I warned you that the gift you desired could not be called back. Once it was set in motion, it could not be stopped. I left you alone since *Walküre*. It was not I, but Fate, that put the temptation before you. It was your own choice to accept it. Now it's all done."

Talia buried her face in her hands and wept disconsolately. When she looked up, the Queen of Spades was gone.

7.

In the third act, Isolde arrives at the castle where the wounded Tristan awaits her. When she arrives, Tristan tears the dressings from his wounds, staggers, and dies in her arms. Talia played the scene with quiet desolation, re-visiting the sight of Armand dying in her arms just as they rejoined. Soon thereafter, she bent over Tristan's corpse and began singing the Liebestod: "*Mild und leise wie er lächelt...*"

When she approached the aria's climax, a feeling of completeness set upon her soul, for she finally understood that her life and her music were meant to be one and the same; the joys and tragedies in one would have to be the same in the other, with or without the help of a witch. And that was fine.

As the final notes of the aria faded away, Talia folded herself over the body of her lover and died as she always had wished: departing life, quite fulfilled and in peace with herself—a great artist done at the completion of her final role.

Lung Replacement

New beginnings are often disguised as painful endings.
- Lao-Tzu

I

"But the lab is heavily guarded," objected Ivan as he tapped with his index finger on the diagram showing the installation's security outposts. "More like a friggin' prison."

"Have no fear," I replied. Ivan was an accomplished killer but was dumb as a rock. "Everyone gets to help with the unloading when a new shipment arrives. We'll sneak in unnoticed, right through here." I traced a path from the woods outside the labs to the western entrance. "I know where to look, and we'll be out before anyone realizes we've paid a visit."

"All the same, it seems very risky to me," countered Ivan mulishly.

I have little patience and can't suffer sniveling from underlings. I am short and stocky, but my voice carries a lot of authority. I didn't get to be head of one of the largest drug cartels in Texas by putting up with the sort of crap Ivan was dispensing.

"Well, you don't have to do it if you are so scared," I replied, letting my annoyance show. "For what I'm paying you, I could get five guys who wouldn't think twice before rushing to help me."

Ivan was a big man, but he cowered easily. "It's not that

I'm scared," he said. "It's that I wish there was a safer way of getting this done."

"That's the way it is," I responded sharply. I had a prolonged fit of coughing and paused to catch my breath. "Now, are you in or out?"

"I s'pose I'm in," sighed Ivan.

II

It was a stupendous coincidence, or a cruel trick of the Fates, that the global famine caused by the extreme environmental degradation had reached a critical stage at the same time the Wilkinson's plague pandemic broke out. Wilkinson's ravages the brains and nervous systems of its victims, leaving the flesh and other organs intact. Therefore, the disease's victims have become a welcome addition to the food baskets of the world.

Thus "walking zombies"—hordes of starving men, women, and children—have become a major safety concern, and the armies of all countries, large and small, have switched from threatening each other to focusing on curbing the incursions of the hungry mobs into hospitals, mortuaries, and cemeteries where one could find Wilkinson's freshly dead, those nearly so, and even those already infected but not quite ready to become entrees.

Cannibalism is still outlawed everywhere, but the governments of the more affluent nations have redirected funds from the maintenance of public order to the procurement and off-the-record distribution of bodies to food kitchens where once chicken, beef, and fish, now almost gone, had been given out.

With public monies dwindling and sources of supply exhausted, it was a godsend that China began selling its dead citizens to a hungry world. Of course, as demand grew, so increased the prices, and the cost of a freshly harvested Chinese disease victim had more than doubled in the three years after the Guangdong outbreak.

Under less compelling circumstances, the Wilkinson's

plague could have had a silver lining, for the availability of fresh corpses would have made more hearts, livers, lungs, and other scarce organs available to the medical community to prolong the lives of their patients. Alas, the care required to preserve those organs in a usable condition made it uneconomical to pursue their collection and distribution except out of specialized facilities. The Opelousas Medical Center, right on the Gulf waterfront a few miles north of Lafayette Island, was one such facility, providing skilled specialists and hard-to-find organs to meet the needs of the affluent sick. This was the place that I'd chosen for our heist.

Why Opelousas? The Center had always been a renowned institution, and its waiting list of those seeking a transplant ran into years. But as legally available organs for transplants became scarce, a community of unscrupulous physicians developed around the center. Skilled surgeons had relocated inland, many of them to Opelousas, after the demise by flooding of five major coastal cities: New York, Boston, Miami, New Orleans, and Houston. These specialists plied their talents on the rich without asking the provenance of the organs involved. As long as there was a match between the organ and the intended recipient and enough money to pay their fees, the doctors would operate, replace organs, and tend to their patients in clandestine facilities. The risks were high, but the fees these doctors charged were astronomical.

I had come from my headquarters in Dallas to Opelousas in search of such rogue practitioners. Back home, a doctor had told me that I had advanced smoking-induced lung disease and might not see Christmas. A second opinion was that I would be lucky to make it to Thanksgiving. Whatever the holiday, the message was clear: if I didn't get a lung transplant in the immediate future, it was curtains.

Money is no object. My drug trafficking operation is quite profitable. I have no moral scruples of any kind, having lost them after the death of my parents and living in a series of foster homes, in which everything that was prohibited happened all the time. Family—wife, kids, relatives—I have none. The only thing I have, and didn't want to lose, was my life. It has always been my intent to hang on to life as long as possible.

I searched around Opelousas until I found a cardiothoracic surgeon who was willing to perform a complex double lung transplant on me, assuming there was a suitable donor. But as the doctor explained, he and the patient had to be willing to accept major risks: the patient of death from the surgery or from organ rejection, and he of losing his license and doing time. So there had to be serious money involved. I gladly agreed to provide it.

Now came the hard part: finding a suitable pair of lungs. Here, the Center might provide the answer. Vessels arrived almost daily at the Opelousas harbor, bringing recent Wilkinson's fatalities in refrigerated containers. If I was lucky, I could get an already preserved pair of lungs at the Center. Failing that, I would have to obtain a fresh body and have the doctor do the lung removal. The doctor agreed to undertake the second course of action only if necessary, at a significantly higher fee because it involved a higher degree of criminal liability.

Through my underground contacts, I met and was able to bribe a venal orderly at the Center, who provided me with a map of the facilities and information on where the organs were stored. He also tutored me on how to decipher the markings on the containers that specified the age, sex, blood type, and harvesting date of the organs. I paid him a ton of money but made a mental note to get rid of him once the transplant operation was done.

III

The arrival schedules of vessels bringing bodies were closely guarded secrets and were irregular because they depended on the vagaries of the spread of the Wilkinson's plague. The epidemic had already spread to the Congo and was beginning to show up in Angola; it was expected to reach South Africa within days. It was not the first time, nor would it be the last, that bands of people driven senseless by hunger or in desperate need of an organ transplant would risk arrest in an attempt to secure arriving corpses to harvest their bodies.

Ivan and I spent two boring days camping in the woods outside the Center, watching for signs of new activity. Finally, on the late afternoon of the third day, there was a stir at the Center, as trucks were readied and dispatched, personnel assembled, steel warehouse doors lifted, and orderlies and nurses in the distinctive teal uniforms of the institution buzzed from one corner of the site to another. Near sunset, closed trucks rumbled on toward the warehouse, and a cordon of men with automatic weapons gathered around the doors to protect the entrance from interlopers.

I squeezed Ivan's shoulder to signify it was time to move, and as the last rays of the sun illuminated the entrance, he jimmied the lock with practiced ease and pushed the west side door open. Inside it was dark, and confused noises reverberated on the walls coming from distant locations in the building. Ivan extracted an LED lamp from his jacket and turned it on, casting a feeble light on the walls and floor of the corridor. We traveled it until it dead-ended in an intersecting corridor.

"To the left," I whispered.

Several turns later, we entered an amphitheater whose walls were covered with floor-to-ceiling refrigerators. In the middle of the room were four identical beds, currently empty but clearly used as dissection tables. Around the tables were stainless steel working stations complete with sinks and a series of glass-fronted storage units that held equipment and supplies. There was a pervasive odor of disinfectant.

I walked up to the refrigeration units. The surgeon had explained that prior to being removed from a donor, lungs are flushed free of blood with a preservation solution that contains electrolytes and nutrients. The lungs, in partially inflated state, are then placed in a temperature-controlled polyurethane container, refrigerated, and transported to the organ depository. What we needed was to find where lungs were stored and locate a set of lungs that were as fresh as possible, were of the same blood type as mine, and hopefully—for this could not be determined in the field, pre-operation—were not too large for my chest cavity. But since I'm a barrel-chested man, I expected that shouldn't be a problem.

After frantically looking at the refrigeration units containing harvested lungs, I came upon a container with the desired label. Those lungs had come from the greater Kinshasa area of the Democratic Republic of the Congo and belonged to a thirty-year-old male who had succumbed to Wilkinson's plague. His organs had come three days ago in the last vessel arriving at Opelousas and had been brought to the Center for transplants. His blood type—oh joy—was A+, same as mine.

"We are in business," I exclaimed. "Let's get out of here."

I extracted the container from the refrigeration unit, and we headed out of the amphitheater.

Midway down the first corridor, however, there sounded a peremptory voice.

"Stop! What are you doing here?"

The bright light of a flashlight nearly blinded me. It was a guard who had come into the corridor from a nearby bend and was pointing a gun threateningly at us. I froze, but Ivan's reaction was instantaneous. He drew a butcher knife from his waistband and, in a single fluid motion, threw it at the guard, hitting him squarely in the chest. The guard tottered and fell to the ground without time to shoot the gun.

"Now we've done it," lamented Ivan, extracting the knife from the guard's bleeding chest and wiping the blade on the victim's uniform. "We better run."

"Wait one second," I reminded him. "This may be to my advantage. Do you think you can drag this man with us until we get back to the car? I can't help you because I need to carry the canister."

"I guess so," replied Ivan. "The guy is smallish. But we must hurry before they come looking for him. Plus, he's bleeding like a gored pig."

"Let's roll."

Thanks to the ongoing operations on the other side of the complex, we managed to exit by the same west entrance without detection. We ran, crouched, each carrying or dragging an important weight. We managed to make it to the woods abutting the Center. From there to the pickup truck parked in a ditch at the side of the road was only a short sprint.

I opened the truck's back gate so that Ivan could place the guard in the truck bed. The bleeding had been reduced to a trickle. As he dropped the body on the truck, the apparent corpse shuddered slightly.

"Damn!" cried Ivan hysterically. "He's still alive!"

"Let's get out of here *now*!" I shouted.

We got in the truck and drove—no, *flew* away as fast as the thing would run.

IV

The doctor was taken aback by our arrival at his door.

Before he could ask any questions, I demanded, "Quick, get a stretcher. We have a dying man in our truck. He could be a potential donor."

"Right," he replied and disappeared inside the office complex.

He returned a short while later pushing a surgical stretcher. "You are lucky there is nobody else here tonight," he observed.

I shrugged. "I also brought a pair of lungs that appear to meet the specs," I said, pointing to the canister. "Where do we go from here?"

"First, let's put that canister under refrigeration right away." The doctor seized the canister and disappeared again. Upon returning, he told us, "Now let's see what we got." He took the guard's arm and felt for a pulse. "He's dead."

After another trip inside, he returned with a collection syringe and, without a word, bent over the cadaver, found a suitable vein in the right arm, and drew a measure of blood.

He then explained, "We need to check the blood type. Excuse me, this will take a while."

He disappeared again.

When he returned, his face registered disappointment. "You wasted your efforts. We can't use his lungs. He is B+. His blood is incompatible with yours."

"What do we do now?" I asked.

The doctor shrugged. "Back to plan A. We prepare you for surgery and hope the harvested lungs work."

"When can you operate?"

"Sometime tomorrow. I need to do some preparations, plus I'll need to have all my staff here to assist with the procedure, which is complicated. Now you need some rest. Come with me to the pre-operation area."

I turned to Ivan. "Please get rid of this trash," I ordered, signaling to the corpse on the stretcher. "And come back here tomorrow morning for instructions."

V

As I spiraled down into anesthetic unconsciousness, troubling thoughts jumbled into my mind. The donor was from a third-world country, with customs and preferences different from those of civilized people like me. Would the grafting of his lungs into my body debase me? Would I become dumb, lazy, sex-starved... I conjured all the deficiencies that could exist in a foreigner and agonized over whether they would take over and impair my excellent personality. I finally passed into a dream in which I was eating food with my fingers and chewing on strange raw roots and meats. The disgust woke me up, only to fall again into an unquiet slumber.

VI

An eternity later, I awoke. Not all at once, but in fits and starts, each accompanied by sharp chest pain. I had tubes and gadgets everywhere: an IV tube in my right arm, a catheter in the neck delivering fluids and medicines, a tube in the throat leading to the windpipe and connected to a ventilator to help me breathe, a urinary catheter, a chest drainage tube to drain fluid and blood around the lungs, and other unseen things I felt all over my body.

Nurses came in every hour to perform a variety of tasks—turning me from side to side, cleaning my mouth with antiseptics, checking the dressing over the incision site to detect bleeding. As I was hooked to a ventilator, I could not speak and could only shake my head "yes" or "no" in response to the nurse's questions. I was groggy, in pain, and more uncomfortable than I had ever been... but *alive!*

The doctor came once or twice a day after the surgery to check on my progress. He reassured me that the operation had gone well, the transplanted lungs were healthy, and there were no signs of rejection. I would be released in a week or two but would always need a doctor's supervision and home therapy. I nodded as if I agreed.

Get me out of here, I thought, *and I'll take care of myself.*

On the third day after the operation, they removed the tube that went down my windpipe and disconnected the ventilator. The relief was immense, and I could talk again, though with difficulty and in a feeble, raspy voice. That day, Ivan came in and reported on the status of my criminal enterprises, which was essentially normal. Cocaine and heroin still flowed into Texas despite martial law and border skirmishes. I told Ivan to lease me a furnished apartment in Opelousas so I could make any required visits to the doctor. Ivan informed me that the police were investigating the break-in at the Center and the disappearance of the guard but so far had found no clues.

Finally, on the seventh day after my surgery, Ivan wheeled me out of the doctor's facility in a wheelchair. I took a deep breath and drank in the clean morning air through my borrowed lungs. This was living! I was very weak but felt ready for a new beginning. I might take a sabbatical and travel the world. Everything was possible, and it was all so sweet. I loved the new lungs and felt no signs of abnormal behavior. Bless the little donor; his aberrations were not contagious.

VII

On the eleventh day, I got a message from the surgeon asking me to come back for testing. The doctor had been surprisingly quiet the last few days, but he had a very busy practice and our business together was winding down, so there was little need for frequent contact between us. I called Ivan on his cell phone but was routed to voicemail. I left a curt message asking where the hell he was and summoned a taxi.

I was a little surprised when the doctor brought me into his office and closed the door. The first question out of his mouth was strange.

"Mr. Malanzoni, have you been reading the papers lately?"

I smiled dismissively. "I've been resting a lot, sleeping late, watching comedy shows on TV, drinking vino, having generally a good time. I'm enjoying life and don't care much for news these days. What, has the war in the Middle East spread to real countries?"

"How about medical news?"

"What do you mean?"

The doctor grimaced. "There are some troubling stories coming out of Gabon. As you know, the second outbreak of Wilkinson's plague originated there. The international teams helping with the epidemic have discovered that the virus that causes the disease has mutated since the original outbreak in China. It appears now that in at least some cases, the virus invades other organs besides the brain. It infects those organs at the same time it attacks the nervous system but remains latent in the organs for a period of time, and then attacks the organs and breaks loose into the rest of the body. Since the victim has been dead for several days and the body is decomposing, this would normally be unimportant, but..."

I was no fool.

"But what happens to the organs of the Wilkinson's victims that are used in transplants?"

"It's not certain yet, but it appears that those organs could be the source of contagion to the recipients. As of yesterday, all trading in Wilkinson's corpses from Africa has been halted. Stocks are tumbling, and trading in companies like Amheart and Organs Unlimited has been stopped to curb panic selling. It's a mess."

"Well, screw them. How about *me*?"

"Too soon to tell. I want you to check into our facility so we can keep you under observation. Wilkinson's symptoms appear without warning, and when they do, death follows quickly."

"But if I'm infected, what can you do for me?"

"Nothing, I'm afraid. At this point, there is no known cure."

"Then what's the point?"

"We can at least give you a comfortable death."

"Never mind comfortable!" I howled. "I'm calling Ivan so he can take me home."

The doctor looked at me askance. "Hmmm... that's something else. A couple of days ago, they found the guard. Ivan had dumped the body in a canal, and it resurfaced. Ivan's DNA markers were all over the corpse, plus others that may be yours or mine or both."

"Where is he now?"

"Ivan is in custody, under interrogation. Let's hope he does not give us away."

"Well, Doctor, that's your problem. It doesn't seem as if they can do squat to me anymore."

So instead of fleeing to the relative safety of Dallas, I went to my apartment and waited for death to arrive. Each day I felt a little worse but could not tell if the disease was taking over or my nerves were betraying me. I'd never been good at coping with adversity.

I was still waiting and fretting when the police came and carted me away.

I mounted a spirited defense with the best lawyers that money could buy. However, Ivan's confession was damning; the bastard had copped a plea and had sung like a canary. Plus, what they called the "circumstantial evidence" was overwhelming. I was convicted of the death of the guard and sentenced to death by lethal injection.

Now I sit in my prison cell awaiting execution tomorrow at dawn. So far, the secondhand lungs from the African victim have served me faithfully. I expect that if I have any last-minute bodily failures, they won't come from them.

FIVE COWRIES

From now on,
I don't care if my tea leaves spell 'Die, Ron, Die,'
I'm chucking them in the bin where they belong.
- J.K. Rowling, *Harry Potter and the Order of the Phoenix*

1

As a cook, Tomasa Bacán was a disaster. Her main dish was a mixture of boiled root vegetables, like yuca and malanga, supplemented by chicken feet, necks, livers, and other offal. She also knew how to make a tasteless okra stew, a non-descript plantain *fufú*, and a pallid *sancocho* whose only flavor came from the large quantities of chili peppers she dumped in the soup.

Evaristo Bulunga could barely down the food she prepared, and that was the source of the first major fight between the newlyweds. After the fourth or fifth sancocho, he protested. "Tomasa, my dear, can you make anything else?"

"Evo, forgive me, but mammy taught me how to sew and wash and iron, but never got around to giving me cooking lessons. The little I know I learned by watching our maid fix her own lunches."

"Do you think that if I get you some goat meat you will be able to prepare a *chilindrón* for me?"

"What's that?"

"Goat creole in spicy tomato sauce. It's my favorite."

"I wouldn't know how to make it."

"You could ask your mother."

"She almost does not talk to me since our wedding. My family doesn't approve of our marriage, you know."

"And your lady friends?"

"They all have given up on me. That is, all except Eulalia, but she knows nothing about cooking, either."

"Couldn't you get a recipe somewhere, maybe in the public library in Sagua? At least you know how to read; you ain't illiterate like me."

"All right, I'll see how I can find a recipe." But she never did, for fear of venturing to try cooking difficult dishes, so she went on serving the tasteless sancochos.

Evaristo would complain to his friends, between gulps of burning rum and puffs of a cheap cigar. "You know me. I'm a simple guy. I like cock fights, playing dominoes and dice, and women with nice hips. I eat anything but would kill for chilindrón. I'm not getting none of the things I like at home."

One or another of the friends would reply something along these lines: "We all warned you. She's wrong for you. She's skinny, almost white, can read and write. She's too high and mighty for you, an illiterate lumberjack. What made you fall in love with her is beyond me."

Evaristo would confess sheepishly, "I dunno. I thought she would be good in bed."

To which the inevitable follow-up question would be, "Well, is she?"

Evaristo would blurt, "She was fine at first. But after a few months, she seemed to lose interest and just lay there as if she didn't care. I've got enough fire for both of us, but I am gettin' turned off by her lack of interest. The worst part is, much as I've tried, I haven't been able to get her pregnant, and I want kids!"

2

Two years into their marriage, Evaristo started going out with his cronies every night to drink rum and play dice. He would stumble back to the *bohío* in the early morning hours, barely conscious. Sometimes he would leave the hut after dinner and would not be back until the following day; occasionally he would be gone for two or three days.

The night of their fifth wedding anniversary found them sitting across each other at the dinner table. Evaristo was sober for a change, staring blindly at the empty wall in front of him. Tomasa's face was puffy and reddish as if she had just finished crying. They stared silently at each other for a long time, as if neither dared start the conversation. At large, Evaristo swallowed hard and started.

"Tomasa, this ain't living. We can't stay like this. I'm going to get us a divorce."

Tomasa uttered a harsh gasp as if squelching a sob. "Evaristo, I don't believe in divorce. I beg you, let's try some other way of dealing with things."

"What are we going to do? The years are piling up. I wanna enjoy life in the time that's left."

"Please," replied Tomasa, choking. "Why don't we give it a try, make an effort to get past our problems, let bygones be bygones?"

"What do you want us to do?"

"Maybe take a vacation, try a change of pace, something that will make us feel better."

"A vacation, where?" asked Evaristo skeptically. "And how is we going to pay for it?"

"Let's go to La Habana. I've been saving all these years for a layette for when our daughter Odalys is born, but she isn't arriving in the near future. Better to invest that money in ourselves, and if kids do come, we'll figure out what to do."

"I didn't know we had any money. I've never been anywhere, not even Holguín, let alone the Capital. I don't know anyone there and wouldn't know where to go."

"Don't you remember my cousin Caridad, the one I mentioned to you several times? She lives near La Habana. She has offered to put us up. Other than transportation, the cost of the trip won't be all that much."

"I don't know, I don't like them adventures. I'm a country folk and cities scare me."

Tomasa let out a short derisive laugh.

If Evaristo had not been such a dark man, his face would have turned all red. Instead of visibly showing embarrassment, he shook his shoulders and replied tentatively, "I'm not leaving this place without a consultation. Many things can happen if we venture out far on them roads."

"Mmmm...." replied Tomasa. "Fine, although I don't believe in *consultas*. But if we are going to do it, we should cast the cowries, as Yemayá, the Great Mother of the Yorubas, teaches. Yemayá invented the use of the shells of sea snails to divine the future."

Evaristo rejected resorting to Yemayá to judge the matter. "No, I don't trust the words of women, which are always false. We better go to a Santería priest of Ogún, the *orisha* who rules metals and tools, and war. The priests of Ogún are serious people."

Tomasa pursed her lips in displeasure, but she gave into his choice. "Well, you go and find in Sagua a santero of Ogún, and in the meantime, I'll write Caridad to start planning the trip."

3

As it turned out, after searching through Sagua de Tánamo's eighteen neighborhoods, Evaristo was unable to find an Ogún santero to handle their consulta. He had, therefore, to settle for a santero of Eleguá, who is the orisha to whom many consultas are directed. Evaristo did not like the change, because the adepts of Eleguá have a reputation for being unscrupulous. Tomasa reminded him, however, that those engaged in reading the cowries have a duty to faithfully interpret what the orishas say, not what is profitable for the reader or preferable to the one making the consultation. Thus, they agreed to consult an Eleguá reader.

The reader they selected came recommended by a Changó *Babalawo* for whom Evaristo had high regard. The reader's home was in the Naranjo Agrio district, on the road from Sagua to Guantánamo. Evaristo and Tomasa went there on an early Monday morning, astride Isabel the mule.

The house in question was a wooden affair with a thatched roof. For a city person, it might have seemed like a poor man's dwelling, but to Evaristo, who was used to living in a bohío with earthen floors, it appeared almost like a mansion. However, the décor inside the house was strange. The walls were covered with dark red paint, and the readings were made on a large ebony table covered by a variety of objects, including jingle bells, a guayaba cane, *maracas* painted red and black, and a pile of small copper coins.

They were met at the door by the reader, who announced that his name was Edelmiro, "but everyone calls me Pupo." He was a light-skinned mulatto of medium height and precise movements, with hair that would have been kinky were it not rendered straight by an ointment that released an acrid smell. He wore black pants and a crimson jacket, as well as a tall, red hat adorned with seashells. He wore a wooden necklace of large, alternating red and black beads.

Pupo asked them whether they had come for a consulta. Evaristo answered respectfully, "Yes, Your Eminence. We're planning an important trip and want to know if the omens for it are good."

Pupo answered right away, rapidly. "You did well in coming here. As you surely know, Eleguá is the prime orisha; he owns all roads and rules all destinies, he opens or closes the astral plane bringing happiness or misfortune to human beings. He must be considered before undertaking anything. He is the doorkeeper for all travels, whether for pleasure or driven by need." He said all of this without a pause as if repeating a well-practiced speech.

Tomasa clarified. "Our trip is one of pleasure, but it is very important to us."

Pupo closed his eyes and stated, in the same manner as before, "Then we must follow the *Eleguá Alá Lu Banshé*, which is the path of Eleguá that rules destiny. On that path, the orisha rules and is lord over all that is planned, the situations that may come up, and the actions that might be taken. Let us pray that Eleguá will lead us to good fortune on that path."

Then, in a different tone, he asked Evaristo, "What offerings do you bring before the orisha?"

"We are poor, and all we have is a *jutía* that I trapped the other night," replied Evaristo, opening a bag to display the corpse of a large rodent whose head was crushed and bloody. "They told me that a jutía is one of Eleguá's favorite offerings."

Pupo did not hide his distaste, and replied in a cutting voice, "Generally, for an important consulta like this one, the offering is a goat or at least a couple of chickens. I'm not sure Eleguá will be pleased with yours."

"We have no money for that," answered Tomasa tartly. "If our offering is not sufficient, I guess we'll have to leave." She had turned towards the door when Pupo replied, "It's not an ideal offering, but maybe Eleguá will look at you with compassion. Let's go ahead with the consulta."

"Thanks, Your Eminence, many thanks," said Evaristo.

"Let me explain briefly how we are going to proceed," continued Pupo, assuming a professorial tone. "I've already purified myself, so I'll now pray to Eleguá to seek his guidance." Without more, he took two steps toward an altar at the back of the room that contained an image of the orisha and intoned reverently, "*Laroyé Eleguá!*" Then he spilled a bit of water on the board where he would cast the shells and called out, "*Omí tutu Ana tuto Tutu larolle Tutu ilei,*" which he translated as, "fresh water to purify the house."

Then he took from the altar several small shells from sea snails and, turning toward the couple, explained, "Eleguá calls for twenty-one cowries, although in a consulta we use only sixteen, which are called the *Dilogún*, and the rest are the *Adele*, which are set aside to serve as witnesses to the reading. Each cowry has an open side and a closed back side, and when I throw them, if the open side is showing one says that the cowry is talking. Only the cowries that talk matter to the reading. I can cast all sixteen, but I am qualified to read the message from only the first twelve. The rest can only be interpreted by a *Babalawo*, who is not present today. I will cast the cowries twice, to make sure to get a precise reading."

Saying that, he shook twelve shells within his hands and dropped them on the board. Five cowries were shown open. He picked up the cowries carefully, enclosed them in his hands, and after shaking them cast them one more time. Again, five cowries talked. With a deep frown, Pupo whispered, "*oshé melli.*"

Evaristo and Tomasa said in unison, "What does that mean?"

"Normally, one would need to prompt the orisha for further clarity by doing an additional throw using an *igbó.*"

"And what is that?" cut in Evaristo, exasperated.

"An igbó is a method for determining whether the answer to the original question asked of the orisha is yes or no; that is, whether the prediction made by the shells is positive or negative. But in this case, the answer is clear, and it is not good. Five and five, '*oshé melli,*' means bad news, death, destruction. Blood will run; the doctor will come. Eleguá says that one of you two, or both, will face a grave risk of death if you take your trip."

Evaristo and Tomasa looked at each other apprehensively. Tomasa had turned pale and was starting to tremble. Evaristo woodenly asked, "Is there anything that can be done about this?"

"I'm afraid not," replied Pupo, but his voice had an evasive tone. At a glance, Evaristo concluded that Pupo was not willing to do anything else for just the price of a jutía. "If you want, I can recommend another reader or a *Babalawo* who can give you a more detailed reading."

"Thanks, we'll think about it," replied Tomasa and turned her back on him.

4

The moment Pupo had closed the door, virtually on their faces, the argument began. Tomasa was disdainful. "We should pay no attention to this Pupo, who's just a charlatan."

Evaristo was dubious. "As you said, he is a man of the gods and is bound to tell the truth. We need to get another consulta."

"Not on your life. I have no more money left to throw away on superstitions."

After that, Tomasa gave Evaristo no peace. She went to the Sagua de Tánamo City Hall to use its phone to call Caridad long distance, and Caridad reiterated that she would receive them with open arms whenever they showed up. Tomasa started to make trip preparations, asking her cousins to come from time to time to feed Isabel, the chickens, and the pig, which they were fattening for Christmas. She went back to Sagua to ascertain the train schedules and bought herself a new dress, modest but well-tailored, to wear on the trip.

After a lot of hard thinking, Evaristo was able to boil the problem down to three questions. First, were the results of the consulta trustworthy? Second, was the foretold catastrophe inevitable, or was it just a possibility that might not take place? Third, and most difficult, did he dare take a chance with Tomasa's life?

None of the questions had an easy answer. He did not trust the oracles of Eleguá, that most dishonest god, particularly when Pupo had behaved in such a shifty manner. On the other hand, he had been able to confirm that the result they had obtained by the casting of the cowries pointed to the existence of a grave danger. He concluded that the most responsible thing was to assume that the reading was legitimate and so was the prediction of a great impending disaster.

The second question was complicated by not knowing whether the results of the throwing of the shells were totally determinative or only indicative of a possibility that could be avoided. He also did not know if the danger was already there or would occur only if they were to go on that trip, so that it could be avoided by staying home. He finally surmised that since they had made a consulta with reference to a planned trip, the more conservative course of action—that is, the least risky—was to stay home.

But then there was the third question. He did not mind so much putting his life at risk, but how about hers? His feelings towards his wife were conflicted. He was certain that he did not love her anymore, indeed could hardly stand her, but what would happen if they took the trip and she died? Could he undertake the trip in the unacknowledged hope that something bad would happen to her? And if it did, could he live with the guilt?

He concluded it was his duty to protect his wife from coming to harm. After four days and nights of mental torture, he made a final decision: give up on the trip, hoping that it would be the best alternative.

Tomasa became unhinged when he announced his decision. "You are an ignorant and a savage. A superstitious fool who believes what a charlatan dressed like a candy bar tells him. If you want to stay, you'll stay alone. I no longer want to go anywhere with you. Tomorrow I will return to my parents' home and from there I will go to La Habana by myself."

Evaristo tried to explain the reasons for his decision, but Tomasa stomped on the dirt floor so hard that earth flew everywhere and screeched, "I'm willing to take my chances! I want this vacation more than anything I ever wanted! If you don't agree for us to go, I won't stay another day with you. I will now go to my parents' home, and I'll divorce you."

Evaristo was taken aback by the vehemence of Tomasa's demands. He racked his brain for a proper response and finally came up with this: "Are you willing to risk your life just to take this vacation?"

Tomasa emphatically spit her answer. "*Yes!*"

Against his better judgment, Evaristo conceded. "All right. We'll go. But don't blame me if anything bad happens."

"Don't worry, I won't."

5

The trip to La Habana was uneventful. Tomasa enjoyed herself tremendously, spending hours chatting with her cousin Caridad, pacing through the broad avenues lined with ceibas and blooming framboyans, gaping at the mansions of the sugar barons, visiting parks, stores, and museums, walking along the seawall, and filling her lungs with pure, salty air.

Evaristo did not enjoy the trip at all. Every minute of the vacation he fretted about the impending disaster the gods had predicted. Not even the delights of Caridad's cooking—she made for him a chilindrón that was fit for a king—could dispel the gloom that enveloped him. He hardly slept during that week and when he did, he woke up every hour with a start, as if an apparition was lurking in the shadows.

When they went back to Sagua, things went back to normal, perhaps even more dismally than before the vacation.

They came to terms with their situation a couple of weeks after their return. She was the one who reopened the topic, during a meal in which Evaristo hardly touched another of her sancochos.

"I still think the vacation was a good idea. It's a pity it didn't work."

"No, it didn't," replied Evaristo curtly.

There was a long silence, and Tomasa ended the conversation and the marriage. "Tomorrow I'm going to Sagua to start work on the divorce papers. Rather than coming back here, I'll stay with my parents."

Evaristo nodded his assent. "Fine by me."

Evaristo left to see his friends while she packed, so he missed her getting on Isabel and trotting to the town to meet with a notary about their divorce and then to her family.

6

It was only a few days later that Evaristo learned that the fish with which the family had toasted Tomasa on her return home were infected with the cigüatera toxin. Tomasa's parents, brothers, and sisters-in-law all came down with diarrhea, vomiting, numbness, dizziness, and weakness, and were very ill for some time, but recovered. Alas, Tomasa sank into a coma from which she never emerged.

The news of Tomasa's death left Evaristo with renewed doubts. "Was it my fault that Tomasa had died due to my giving in and agreeing to take the trip? But if we had stayed home and not left for Havana, would it not have somehow ended the same way? Maybe the dangerous travel was not the one to Havana, but Tomasa's return to her family?"

After a while, Evaristo told himself, "I better stop wasting my time like this. The fact is that Tomasa has disappeared from my life, and I'm free again!"

He finished a cigar and went out to join his drinking buddies.

7

Evaristo did not stay in mourning long. In a few weeks, he met a dark, earthy woman much like himself, with generous hips, a good cook, endowed with a loud voice and infectious laughter. It is unclear whether they married, but all the same, she bore him six healthy children who filled the bohío with their joyous noise.

Evaristo never strayed away from Sagua for even a mile, and he had no occasion or desire to consult the gods about anything again.

TIGER BY THE TAIL

He was in the predicament of a man who had got a tiger by
the tail –it was neither safe to hold nor let go.
Chinese proverb (paraphrased)

He circled the display table three times before he
made up his mind. Among the countless drawings,
portraits, pictures of angels, demons, shepherds,
maidens, and other objects of diverse shapes and
colors, he finally selected a hand-sized blue ensemble that
appeared to represent a boy, the head a tad too large but
otherwise finely carved, holding onto the tail of some unrecognizable animal, threateningly turned towards its cap-
tor. He carefully picked up the bauble and declared, "I
guess I will do this one."

The Proctor shrugged. "Well, I will enter it in the ledger.
Remember, you have one week to do an analysis of the candidate and submit a report. Next Monday, by noon."

The Examiner looked again at the lapis lazuli lump of
carved stone and read the tag dangling from a cord on the
animal's neck. "Vanessa Lynn. # 34887-C. Chatham
House." He sighed.

As an upper-class man, it was his chore of interviewing
potential candidates for admission into the Art School. He
hated this. Ninety-five out of a hundred times, he had to
hand out disappointment to worthy, but not worthy
enough, applicants. It was not fair. But of course, he had
made it in three years ago even though his skills as an ab-

stract painter were middling. He should not be complaining.

* * *

"Why do you want to enter the Art School?" He was mechanically going through the list of questions. The girl's unseeing eyes were aimed at a spot on the back wall of her small apartment.

"That should be obvious," she replied. "What job can a blind girl aim for, when all the skills she has are on the tips of her fingers?" There was bitterness and defiance in her reply.

"But most art forms are unavailable to you, Miss Lynn. Even as a sculptor, your range of activities would be limited. You would not be able to do large bronzes, and even man-sized work may be denied you because your subjects might refuse to let you touch them with the frequency and intimacy that is required. And...."

She interrupted him, not trying to disguise her scorn. "I am not the first, or only, blind person who has succeeded as a sculptor. Think of Tagliaferri, Ellis, Naranjo, many others. And I can not only sculpt, but I do wood carvings, textiles. It is only the prejudice of the seeing ones that keep us back."

"That is all well and good, *signorina*. But why should the greatest art school in the world give up one of the few available places in this year's class to someone who admittedly has a serious handicap that would require extra care and attention, and whose prospects as an artist are dubious?"

Vanessa frowned, but her answer shot out like a dart. "First, because I am better than most of your applicants, as you must have noticed. Second, because I am sure my name will add luster to your school's fading reputation. And third, because I am a woman and a blind one at that; you guys owe me."

It was the Examiner's turn to frown. "Fading reputation?

How do you mean?" This interview was going nowhere fast.

Again, the reply came without hesitation. "Come now, sir. There have been at least three major scandals concerning your faculty and students in the last five years. You are a favorite of the tabloids. Donations are dropping; it is all over the papers. Sexism is one of the lesser sins of which you stand accused." Her voice had climbed until it was almost a shriek.

The Examiner stopped to consider what his next question should be. "What makes you think you are better than the other applicants?"

Her answer was prompt. "You have in your possession my study of a boy and a tiger. The boy I carved from my next door neighbor's son. Obviously, I have not been able to touch a tiger. Isn't that good enough to get me in?"

The Examiner opened his satchel. The boy was indeed finely rendered: expressive face showing stress and puzzlement, straining arms, bulging chest muscles, feet tightly planted on the base of the sculpture. The animal, though, was something else: a large, misshapen lump with four stubby extremities and a cavern of a head from which protruded rows of sharp teeth. "Couldn't you have done better on the tiger? Maybe used a cat as a model?"

This time she hesitated a second before replying. "The tiger can be anything. One's fears and emotions, the threats of the world, the vagaries of ill luck. There is only one boy; there are many tigers."

"That may be as you say, but as it is, what I am holding is an imperfect work that does not fully show what talent you possess."

For the first time, there was a touch of doubt in her answer. "Well, let me prove it to you."

"How? I am only allowed to judge based on the sample you submitted."

The girl took a deep breath and said in a low voice, "Let me do a sculpture of your head. I can have it ready by

Thursday. If it does not satisfy, you can give me a bad report."

The Examiner shook his head vigorously. "That is totally outside the rules. If you succeeded in persuading me that way, it would be unfair to every other candidate."

She was almost crying now. "Fair? What is fair? Is being born blind fair? Is being born a woman fair? Is it fair that you can't understand what it means to be faced with these tigers?"

The familiar pain struck him again. Why did he have to be the one to crush another person's hopes? Why couldn't the faculty do this? This was of course another test that the students at the Art School had to go through in order to graduate. He sighed.

She heard the sigh and brightened up at once. "See, you know it is not fair. Why don't you give me a chance to prove myself to you?"

"I don't count. You might as well try to convince a fruit seller down the road."

"It counts for me. If I convince you, I will at least feel somewhat vindicated."

He pondered at this for a long moment. Finally, he shrugged his shoulders and said, "So be it. I will let you do a sculpture of my head. But it will not count officially toward my report. I will have to base it on your boy with a tiger by the tail."

"Thank you very much. When can we start?"

* * *

He was amazed at how quickly she worked. Just two sittings, Tuesday and Wednesday, and a model was done. She had gone over his face many times, as if trying to memorize his every feature, even the frown that betrayed his uneasiness. He looked at the misshapen lump of clay and could not recognize any part of him. Was she some kind of fraud?

Late Thursday night a boy delivered a message. Just three

words. "It is ready."

* * *

Friday morning found him at the door of her Chatham House apartment. He could not hide his curiosity. While the girl seemed talented, her technique baffled him. Not that it mattered; it would have to be great for him to ever pay attention to it.

She opened the door at the second knock and ushered him into the small living room. "Just one moment, please," she said as she retreated into what was probably both her studio and bedroom. "Please take a seat."

The Examiner lowered himself into an armchair and readied himself to wait. But the wait was short: soon Vanessa returned, holding an object under a stained piece of cloth. "Here it is," she announced, placing the object on a small table by the armchair. With a flourish, she peeled away the cloth and took two steps back.

The Examiner gasped and then remained silent for a very long time. He was staring intently at the small stone bust that contained a miniature rendering of his face. The resemblance was uncanny: it was him, and then it was more than him... The statue captured his features, yes, but it also conveyed ambition, thinly contained rage, envy, ruthlessness... All the feelings that he thought he hid so well, and now lay bare right in the open. He was confused, and then bafflement gave way to alarm: nobody should be allowed to see this, know him as he truly was. His career had not yet taken off, but if this damnable portrait was seen outside this room, it never would. It must be destroyed.

He rose slowly and cleared his throat. "Miss Lynn, this is a fine work. Let me take it with me and ponder over the weekend what light it casts on your application."

As he hurried to the door, her words chased after him. "Thank you, sir. But please take care of that little trinket. I would like to get it back as a reminder of our meetings." Then, after a pause: "In any case, shall depend on your integrity and good judgment."

Was there a touch of irony in her words?

* * *

It was a difficult weekend for the Examiner. Disposing of the bust was not the problem; he had barely arrived at the school workshop when, armed with a heavy hammer, he began destroying the evidence of his true character to bits. The question was what to do about the blind girl's application.

He debated the question in his mind day and night. On the one hand, he was assuredly in the presence of a true and rare genius, one that could bring needed luster to the Art School. However, if admitted she would require extra accommodations due to her handicap, and any inconvenience she might cause could be blamed on him. Also, if she was let in, what prevented her from visiting the same type of mischief upon others in the faculty, or doing other work that was too revelatory to be appreciated? She was clearly dangerous, and whatever ills she brought might be laid at his feet for getting her admitted.

Late Sunday night, he finally decided: he could not let her in. Whatever justice and fairness might have called for, he was going to take no chances with his career. He was aware of his limitations as an artist and the need to curry favor with the faculty. And, behind it all, a little mouse gnawed at his heart, observing, "And she is a much finer artist than you will ever be." He retired and slept through the night.

The following morning, he wrote a short memo to the Admissions Committee, justifying the rejection this way: "*Miss Lynn is a serious artist, who has managed to overcome a severe handicap to create interesting work. Yet her art is uneven, as shown by her clumsy attempt to create an image of a tiger. Admitting her would be a gamble that this school need not make. I recommend she not be admitted.*"

* * *

Years passed. The Examiner became the Dean; the School prospered. Each new incoming class seemed more talented and promising than the previous ones. All was well in the art world.

One Friday morning while thumbing through the announcements in the *Times*' Weekend Arts section, the Dean stumbled upon an advertisement by one of the finest galleries in the city: "The Seven Deadly Sins: Sculptures and Other Works by a Major New Artist, Vanessa Lynn. Opening October 3." The ad included a picture that the Dean knew very well: a teenage boy holding for dear life onto the tail of a misshapen monster.

No doubt, the prudent thing was to stay clear of this exhibition. Yet he could not help himself, and it was with a blend of curiosity and dread that he arrived in the gallery. He was late; the opening reception was winding down, yet there were still attendees milling around. He even knew a few of them. One of the patrons, a desiccated old lady in a gray designer gown, gave him a startled look and muttered something like, "It is you!" before turning away abruptly toward the table holding the white wine and the canapes.

The Dean shrugged and proceeded to examine the sculptures that seemed to crowd the room. He did not get to see very much, though. Against one of the walls, under a banner announcing in oversized characters THE SEVEN DEADLY SINS, there were seven sculptures arranged in a semicircle and one other in front of the rest. His eyes immediately were drawn to the centerpiece, a large version of the familiar boy wrestling with the monster. A placard under the sculpture read: "Man and the Passions that Seek to Overpower Him." Right behind it, bearing the sign "Envy" was a full-size bust of the Dean, as he looked when younger. Despite the age difference, the resemblance was unmistakable, as were the covetousness and jealousy that surfaced over the placid features of the model.

The Dean was in the grip of so many emotions that he failed to notice the approaching steps of someone who drew near, gingerly drawing a cane before her. "It seems to be the favorite of many of the visitors. I am told by the gallery owner that we already got a bid from some foreign bank that wants to display it in the lobby of its main office. Do you remember it, sir?"

The Dean found himself at a loss for words. Finally, he grumbled, "How did you know it was me here?"

"I recognized the cologne you always wear. Cheap, but distinctive."

The Dean finally recovered enough to raise his voice belligerently, "Well, you can't do this. You don't have my permission. It is theft, and defamation to boot. I will sue."

Miss Lynn responded calmly. "I never gave you permission to keep the first version of this. You never gave it back either, and I don't know what happened to it. Luckily, I kept the clay model. Anyhow, good luck with your suit. I am sure the bank will not want to part with what is likely to become a famous piece."

Perhaps it was guilt, or the realization that any action against Miss Lynn, the gallery, or the bank would only bring more unwanted publicity. The Dean turned around and began his retreat. He stopped when a final thought crept onto his mind.

"I wish you had used a cat for your model of the tiger. You probably would have gotten in, and all this unpleasantness would have been avoided."

"I am deathly allergic to cats," said Miss Lynn.

Something in the Water

FBI BROUGHT IN TO INVESTIGATE WAPITI FIRE AND EXPLOSION

Casper Star-Tribune Staff, September 8, 2048. The Park County Sheriff's Office has confirmed that agents from the Federal Bureau of Investigation's Denver Field Office have arrived in Cody to take part in the investigation of the explosion and fire at the Lost Trails Saloon in Wapiti that took the lives of a still undetermined number of people last Wednesday evening. Sheriff Neal Stewart described the FBI presence as a welcome addition to the local and state team that is seeking to unravel the causes of the mysterious event, the deadliest in Western Wyoming since the 1940s. As previously reported, the explosion occurred in the early evening in the middle of the pre-Labor Day week. Because of Wapiti's proximity to the eastern entrance to Yellowstone, the park and the surrounding area has been teeming with holiday visitors, making the work of the investigating team particularly difficult. The Star-Tribune has learned that a potential person of interest is being held for questioning, but no details have been released by the authorities thus far.

* * *

Excerpts from the Transcript of the Interrogation of Joseph Weda
September 5, 2048

Agent Eric Brady, Federal Bureau of Investigation (EB):
      Please state your name for the record.

Joseph Weda (JW):   Joseph Carlos Weda.

EB: How do you spell that?

JW: It depends. The Shoshone word has an H at the end, but in dealing with white people we spell it W-E-D-A.

EB: Mr. Weda, before we started this interview, I apprised you of your Miranda rights and you declined to have an attorney present and agreed to proceed with the interview. Is this correct?

JW: Yes. I don't care for them lawyers.

EB: And you understand that this interview is being taped and a record is being made of the questions and your answers. Is that correct?

JW: Yes.

EB: And that this record may be used in future proceedings?

JW: What's proceedings?

EB: Court cases and the like.

JW: Yes.

EB: Mr. Weda, are you a Native American?

JW: My father was Shoshone, my mother Mexican.

EB: What was your place and date of birth?

JW: Am born on the Wind River Reservation in Fort Washakie, south of here, on November 2, 2023.

EB: What is your current address?

JW: The Lost Trails Saloon in Wapiti.

EB: Where else have you lived since your birth?

JW: I left the reservation when I was thirteen years old, on account there was too much crime there, and my mother sent me to live with her sister in Meeteetse. I stayed there until I graduated from high school in 2041, but there was no work, so I been moving around looking for jobs since that date. I done lived in Dry Creek, Dumbell, Willwood, even here in Cody, and finally got a job at the Saloon and came to Wapiti a couple of years ago.

EB: What was the job that brought you to Wapiti?

JW: Some guys from back East bought the Saloon three years back and began fixing up the place with an aim to reopen it. The Saloon had been shut down for several years and was in bad shape. The new owners put an ad in the Cody Enterprise asking for a live-in server to help with the business and the up-keep of the saloon. The pay was five bucks an hour, and I figured that and the tips and having my meals and housing taken care of, it would be all right... but not... great, you know. So I got my buddy Herman to lend me his pickup and I came out to Wapiti and applied in person and was hired.

EB: Who hired you at the Saloon?

JW: The manager, who was also one of the owners.

EB: What was his name?

JW: I dunno his first name, everyone called him Mr. Inman.

EB: Who were the other owners?

JW: I am not sure who they all were, owing that they kept coming in and out. There was Mr. Sawyer, Mr. Walker, Mr. Bowers, Mr. Miller, Mr. Skinner, and Mr. Yates and a couple of others that I can't much recall.

EB: What do you mean by coming in and out?

JW: Mr. Inman ran me ragged serving tables, cleaning the place, and doing other chores, so I had no time to pay them much heed, but the others showed up every once in a while, in ones and twos, always puttin' on airs. They ate and drank and never paid for nuthin', and just sat in the saloon for hours on end. Mr. Inman was chummy with them and often would sit at their table to share a beer and shoot the breeze.

EB: What did they talk about?

JW: Like I said, I never paid them much mind, I was always busy with one thing or another. It seemed they talked about things that most of the time didn't make no sense.

EB: Did Mr. Inman and the others treat you well?

JW: I reckon'. They never called me "injun" or "half-breed" or anything, and did not hit me or pushed me around all that much. Mr. Inman called me stupid when I did something he didn't like, but that was it.

...

EB: You are not tall and don't seem that strong. Did people mistreat you before you came to work at the Saloon?

(Pause)

EB: Back on the record. While we were off the record, Mr. Weda indicated that he had been the victim of repeated physical and sexual abuse as a youngster, when he lived at the reservation. But to clarify, that did not happen to you while at the Saloon?

JW: No, sir. Like I said, sometimes Mr. Inman said I was kind of thick, like stupid, and he and the others shoved me around a bit, but nuthin' major.

EB: Did you have any complaints about your job at the Saloon?

JW: No, Sir. The pay wasn't that great, and tips were few except in the summer, but I had little expenses and was saving some for when I was to move away, like to California or sumthin'.

...

EB: What was your work schedule?

JW: Eight a.m. to eleven p.m. every day, and got Wednesdays off.

EB: What did you do on your days off?

JW: Herman would usually pick me up and would drive us to Cody. We would walk around and go to the Buffalo Bill Museum or the Gun Museum or one of the other places in town, hang around the stores, you know. He had an apartment, and we would go there in the afternoon and watch TV and have a couple of beers. He would drive me back to the Saloon in the evening so I could get back to work.

EB: How did they manage on Wednesdays while you were off?

JW: The Saloon was closed on Wednesdays. Charlie, the cook, was also off that day.

EB: Was the Saloon also closed this last Wednesday?

JW: Yes, sir.

EB: So, what did you do that day?

JW: Herman came to pick me up early and we drove back to Cody. We had breakfast at Wendy's, which was passing fair, went to the Old Trail Museum, and then had lunch at Annie's and back to Herman's apartment.

EB: How long were you at Herman's apartment?

JW: I guess it been five or six when Herman drove me back to Wapiti.

EB: Wasn't that a little early?

JW: Well, Herman and I sorta had a fight, and he wanted to send me home early.

EB: What was the fight about?
      (Pause)

JW: Er... I reckon' Herman was sorta jealous because I had been much friendly with one of them attendants at the Old Trail Museum.

...

EB: What happened when you went back to the Saloon?

JW: Like I said, the place was closed, and I was upset from my fight with Herman and feeling kinda down, so I let myself in and was on my way back to my room at the rear of the building when I heard sumthin' that seemed like voices, though there was no one in the restaurant. I stopped to track down the noise, which came from near the back wall, where there were a bunch of long tables used for big parties. Only them tables had been moved to the center of the room and the floor had been cleared out. I approached on tippy toes and noticed a trap door on the floor that had always been covered by a rug.

EB: Did you know the trap door was there previously?

JW: No.

EB: Please continue.

JW: I got on my knees and placed my ear against the door to listen. I couldn't make it out well, but then I noticed a heating register, sorta like a grill, a few inches away, and the sounds seemed to be coming out louder through the register. I scooted over and was able to pick up the voices much better.

EB: What were they saying?

JW: I recognized several of the voices, like that of Mr. Yates and also Mr. Inman's. When I started listening, someone, I think it was Mr. Skinner, was givin' a talk.

EB: What was the talk about?

JW: He said he had continued to work with the people at a place called Cold Harbor Laboratory.

EB: Do you mean Cold Spring Harbor Laboratory?

JW: I guess so. He, Mr. Skinner, had guided them to the discovery of a method for replacing sumthin' called the X sumpthin' with a Y summpthin'. I didn't understand what he said, but he repeated twice that by doin' this replacing it would be possible to breed only boys, no girls.

EB: Was he talking about people?

JW: Yessir. I thought he were talkin' about cattle, but I gather from the ways he talked he surely meant peoples.

EB: Did he say how this would work?

JW: He said that Mr. Sawyer had made a chemical that women would take early in their pregnancy, and would have the effect of turning one of those X things of an unborn baby into a Y.

EB: But what if the baby was already bound to be a boy?

JW: That was what the Cold Harbor folks was working on. Them was makin' sumthin' called an inhator that would recognize a boy was cookin' and make the main chemical inactive.

EB: You mean inhibitor?

JW: I dunno. Maybe.

EB: So there were two things in the supplement: a thing that changed the sex of a baby girl into a baby boy, and another that would nullify the effect of the first if a baby boy was being produced?

JW: I dunno.

EB: But why would a National Laboratory want to engage in that kind of research?

JW: Mr. Skinner said he had convinced the Cold Harbor folks that this research would help with the population in countries like India where there were over two billion peoples.

EB: What else did they say?

JW: Mr. Skinner shut up and someone else spoke. I ain't catch who. He had a squeaky voice, but I thunk he said that a factory in Bensenville, near the Off-hair [sic] airport, was done finished and was ready to start mass production. He said he could deliver fifty thousand packs a day and fly 'em out of Off-hair [sic] to all parts of the world. Mr. Walker then said he had peoples in a hundred places to have the stuff given out.

EB: But how were they going to get customers to sign up for the program before it was even made public?

JW: They wasn't no signing up. Mr. Walker said his teams would dump the stuff in the water supply. The chemicals would dissolve in the water and the water would be drunk by pregnant women.

...

EB: What were they trying to accomplish, do you know?

JW: Yeah.

EB: What was it?

JW: When Mr. Walker got finished with his tale, Mr. Yates said like, "We may need to do this several times, but in a generation or two there will be no women left alive. Mankind will disappear from the face of the earth." Mr. Inman added, "Maybe sooner. As men are left on this planet without women, they will turn on each other. There'll be wars, revolutions, all sorts of things. Boys and young men will become slaves and serve the older ones, and many will revolt. It will be great to watch."

EB: What did you think of that?

JW: It was like it happened to me, only much worse. I hated it.

EB: So their purpose was to kill off the entire human race?

JW: Yeah, each and every one of us.

EB: But why would anyone want to do that?

JW: (In a low voice) Because them ain't humans.

EB: What do you mean?

JW: (In a low voice) Them is aliens that want to take over this world without having to fire a shot.

EB: But don't they look human to you?

JW: (In a low voice) They be disguised. I know them disguises.

EB: Have you seen them out of disguise?

JW: No. Wednesday was the first time I found out this was going on.

...

EB: What did you do when you heard this conversation?

JW: I left the Saloon and sat on the ground, in a corner of the parking lot, outta sight from the building, feeling scared and lousy and trying to figure out what to do. I thought of going to the police, but who would believe me, an ignorant redskin from a bar in the middle of nowhere? And I could not confront them, because they would kill me. Then I reckoned I had to get them before them got us.

EB: What did you do?

JW: I knew our stove ran on gas, and there was a line that ran from there to the outside of the Saloon and connected to an underground pipeline. I crept back into the Saloon, went to the kitchen, and with a meat cleaver cut the gas line. I stood at the back exit, waited a while, and threw a match into the escaping gas. I was blown away by the explosion. When I picked myself up, I was bruised and a little burned up, but the entire Saloon was in flames.

EB: So you deliberately set fire to the Lost Trails Saloon, and caused the death of a number of its occupants?

JW: Yeah. None of them roaches escaped, I hope.

EB: And you did this deliberately and with full knowledge that in setting up the explosion and the fire you were likely to cause the death of one or more persons?

JW: You bet.

EB: What did you do after the explosion and the fire?

JW: I was kinda dizzy. I kept on walking in circles 'til the fire truck and the police arrived.

EB: Were you taken into custody then?

JW: Yes, after a while the sheriff arrived and took me into the Detention Center in Cody.

EB: Did they take a sample of your blood at the Detention Center?

JW: I don't recall.

...

EB: Mr. Weda, do you ever consume alcoholic beverages?

JW: Yeah, a bit.

EB: Last Wednesday, when you arrived at the Lost Trails Saloon, how much alcohol had you consumed?

JW: I guess three or four beers, I got thirsty during my

fight with Herman.

EB: And do you use any drugs?

JW: You mean medicines?

EB: No. Hallucinatory drugs or opiates like heroin or cocaine.

JW: Herman and I do meth together, makes our sex more enjoyable.

EB: Last Wednesday, had you taken meth before returning to the Lost Trails Saloon?

JW: Yeah.

EB: How much?

JW: Not sure. Half a gram, maybe.

EB: Is there anything else you want to state for the record at this time?

JW: No.

EB: For the record, this interview was completed on September 5, 2048, at 3:30 p.m., Mountain Daylight Savings Time.

* * *

Excerpt from Memorandum from Agent Eric Brady to Robert Todd, Special Agent in Charge
September 15, 2048

This is a most perplexing case. There is no doubt as to Mr. Weda's responsibility for the events at the Lost Trails Saloon. Not only has he confessed his crime, but our investigation has confirmed that the gas line to the building was deliberately severed and ignited, causing the explosion and the subsequent fire.

Also, a separate interview with a Herman Padilla of Cody has established that he and Mr. Weda had a prolonged homosexual relationship and that there was significant alcohol consumption and drug use during their encounters. Mr. Padilla also confirmed that on Wednesday, September 2, the weekly encounter between Mr. Padilla and Mr. Weda was cut short due to a quarrel between them. Prior to, during, and following that meeting, both of them consumed large amounts of liquor and used a significant amount of methamphetamine. Mr. Padilla believes that when he dropped Mr. Weda at the Lost Trails Saloon, Mr. Weda was highly intoxicated ("high as a kite" were the words he used) and in a foul mood. He said that on the way to Wapiti, Mr. Weda complained, as he often did, about having to go back to that "dump" that he hated because he was "treated there like a dog."

Mr. Padilla, who was visibly irritated at Mr. Weda, also indicated that Mr. Weda had a flair for the dramatic and enjoyed drawing attention to himself. He cited an instance two years ago when Mr. Weda allegedly showed up at the Park County Fair drunk and in disguise, wearing clown makeup, a three-cornered hat, and yellow baggy pants, and proceeded to regale fairgoers with what Mr. Padilla described as "zany tales," although he did not recall what these were about. We could not confirm Mr. Padilla's story. Blood samples taken from Mr. Weda late in the evening of September 2 determined a blood alcohol concentration of 0.2%, more than double the level considered intoxication under Wyoming state law. Likewise, there were significant levels of methamphetamine in his blood.

We also did limited investigations at Wind River and in Meeteetse. Those residents of the Wind River reservation that remember him state that he was a practicing homosexual from an early age and had numerous sexual encounters with older boys and other residents. One interviewee confirmed that Mr. Weda was severely beaten by other boys on more than one occasion. Members of the faculty at the Meeteetse School recall that Mr. Weda was a "hysterical boy" and was regarded as a "pansy" by students and teachers alike.

Based on the foregoing, a strong case can be made for the proposition that Mr. Weda arrived at the Lost Trails Saloon in a highly excited, perhaps hallucinatory, state, that he set the Saloon afire in a fit of anger, and that the conversations that he allegedly overheard were deliberate lies or a fantasy manufactured by his addled mind. In particular, the scheme for depopulating the planet that he describes is highly improbable. One would think advanced aliens would have thought of a more efficient way of doing this.

But please consider the following:

1. There was a secret underground room in the Saloon with a capacity for over a dozen people.

2. A person located on the trap door above the room could listen in on conversations in the underground room through the HVAC register, particularly if those were conducted at elevated voice levels.

3. No recognizable human remains were discovered in the underground room, but many partly melted pieces of a plastic-like substance of unknown composition were strewn throughout.

4. Traces of non-alcoholic beverages, again of unknown composition, were found on the surface of a metal cupboard that was only partially damaged by the fire.

5. No reports of missing persons have been filed since September 2 that match the names or descriptions of the individuals named by Mr. Weda.

6. Real estate records for Park County reflect that the property known as the Lost Trails Saloon was purchased in March 2045 by a Mr. Waylon Inman from New York City. Mr. Inman paid $125,000 for the property, including the saloon and the surrounding five acres of land. According to the sales contract file with the deed, Mr. Inman apparently paid in cash and assumed the title free of any liens or encumbrances. A preliminary review of tax records in New York City finds no entries for any person named Waylon Inman.

7. Wapiti is an isolated community but is so close to the eastern entrance to Yellowstone National Park that it sees a constant inflow of out-of-town visitors. It could be a fine place for hiding in plain sight.

8. There are no assurances that, if a secret cell of aliens like the one described by Mr. Weda existed, there may not be others elsewhere.

9. I did some checking on the internet. I'm not an expert on these kinds of things, but there are articles reporting a slight decrease in the last couple of years in the number of females born in the United States and several Western European countries.

Is it possible that, despite his deranged state of mind and odd proclivities, Mr. Weda may have eavesdropped on a conversation among aliens bent on humanity's destruction? They say that the level of risk is the product of the probability of an event occurring times its anticipated consequences. Here, the story told by Mr. Weda is most improbable, but if true, the consequences of the alleged plot being carried out are devastating. For that reason, I suggest that the scenario described by Mr. Weda presents a level of risk that cannot be ignored and should be investigated.

I therefore recommend that the Bureau at a minimum follow up with the Cold Spring Harbor Laboratory, look into suspicious new industrial activity in the Bensenville, Illinois area, and take such other measures deemed appropriate and prudent.

Signed,

Agent Eric A. Brady

Handwritten note to the margin of the September 15, 2048, memorandum from Mr. Brady to Mr. Todd

Request noted and denied. Preposterous. Archive. Robert Todd, September 16, 2048.

The Sisters of Mercy

Oh the sisters of mercy, they are not departed or gone.
They were waiting for me...
                                          - Leonard Cohen

I t seemed a great investment. My broker, who had a nose for this sort of thing and connections in every industry, said it was a once-in-a-lifetime opportunity not to be missed: investing in a limited partnership just about to go public, seeking to raise capital to establish a rare earth mining enterprise in the Mount Ngualla area of Tanzania. He explained that rare earths are seventeen chemical elements, existing only in relatively small quantities, which are vital to many technologies, including consumer electronics, computers and networks, communications, clean energy, advanced transportation, health care, environmental mitigation, national defense, and many others. At the time, China had a stranglehold on the world's supply of rare earths, but the Ngualla area appeared to hold significant amounts of bastnaesite and synchysite, ores that contain Cerium and several other rare earths.

I did not understand the fine points of mineral extraction and marketing, but it seemed like a good opportunity to make money, and, being single and feeling adventurous, I made a half-a-million-dollar investment and thereby became one of five founding members of the limited partnership. To my delight, the investment proved a veritable gold mine (no pun intended), and within ten years of the start of operations my partnership share was conservatively valued by my accountant at tens of millions of dollars, with an annual income in the high six figures.

All was fine and dandy. But then a strange letter with an overseas return address showed up in my mailbox. It read:

Dear Sir,

You are an investor in a partnership that is exploiting the natural resources of Southwest Tanzania. The inhabitants of that region, particularly those living in the Chunya area, are impoverished and ravaged by deadly diseases including HIV and Rift Valley fever. The enterprise of which you are part does nothing to alleviate the suffering of the people and instead contributes to the health crisis by causing its workers to contract pneumoconiosis and nephrogenic systemic fibrosis from the inhalation of mine dust. It obtained an environmental permit through the bribery of the corrupt Tanzanian government and is allowed to pollute and leave a permanent scar on our beautiful country. It exploits its workers by paying them hunger wages. For the love of God, please cease your nefarious activities. Either reform or shut down your operations in Ngualla now!

The Sisters of Mercy of Tanzania

A Congregation Member of the Mercy International Association

My first instinct was to throw the letter into the wastebasket and forget about it. Upon reflection, though, I decided to alert my partners of the broadside, since it could lead to public relations problems in the future. My inquiries were received with the equivalent of a corporate shrug of the shoulders: Yes, the partnership was aware of the charges, as all the other partners had received similar accusatory letters. The nuns in question were world-famous do-gooders who lacked political or economic clout. Nobody in Tanzania would pay attention to them and responding to their accusations would only give the claims free publicity. The best course of action was to ignore them. And so I did.

A few months went by, and I pretty much forgot about

the complaining nuns. So, the arrival of another letter from abroad took me entirely by surprise. This one was very brief:

> *Sir:*
> *You and your partners continue to operate the Ngualla mines, bringing suffering and despair to the innocent population of Tanzania. You are hereby advised that persisting in your ungodly behavior will have serious consequences for the partnership and its members, yourself included.*
> *Sincerely,*
> *The Sisters of Mercy of Tanzania*
> *A Congregation Member of the Mercy International Association*

I was somewhat cowered by the threat. I called John, the general partner. He was a brusque Irishman with whom I had sharp disagreements in the past, for I did not approve of his dictatorial and exploitative ways of running the enterprise. He replied to my questions about the threat with a series of invectives directed at nosy lesbian nuns, ungrateful savages, and politically correct liberals (perhaps meaning me). He bemoaned the passing of colonialism and ended his tirade by declaring in a huff, "Let them try to do something against us or our facility. I know where to find mercenaries in that part of the world. We'll crush them."

I hung up, tore up the letter, and tossed it into the trash.

The holidays were approaching, and like the rest of the consuming public, I spent inordinate amounts of time making purchases and preparing for upcoming parties. One cold December morning, a large parcel arrived at my bachelor townhouse. It was wrapped in plain brown paper and had no return address. Thinking it was an early Christmas present from one of my aunts, I opened it and found it contained a cardboard box with an elaborate label that read "Tanzania's World-Famous Spice Island Spice Cake." Below the caption, there was a short blurb inviting the purchaser to eat the product by itself, "with your favorite ice cream," or as an accompaniment to "your morning cup of tea or coffee." It also indicated: "Will stay fresh for a week or more if stored unopened." Inside the box, there was an oblong, golden cake redolent of cloves and other exotic spices.

I am not a dessert-loving person, but I could not resist the temptation. I immediately brewed a fresh pot of coffee, placed the cake on a serving platter, sat at my dinette table with a cup of coffee, and sliced a couple of pieces off the dense cake. Immediately, the mass of the cake released scores of tiny eggs that rolled off the top of the table and spread all over the floor of the kitchen. I soon discovered that sweeping them with a broom was largely ineffective since the eggs went into crevices in the floor, under carpets, behind and around the furniture. The vacuum cleaner picked some up, but many remained at large. It was a nuisance.

Two weeks later, the eggs reappeared in the form of metallic-looking flies with big red eyes and orange and black bands across their abdomens. They flew all around the living room, kitchen, and even the bedroom, landing on exposed surfaces. I finally got rid of them with insecticide, and the infestation was soon over.

Unbeknownst to me, however, some of the flies had laid eggs on the bedclothes and on my shirts and other items of clothing. Their presence became evident when, a few days later, the eggs hatched, and the emerging larvae penetrated my body. I experienced unbearable itching, and boil-like lesions began covering me; I could see maggots crawling under the skin and even across my eyelids. Each lesion became an infected, raised spot with clear fluid oozing out of a hole in the middle of the boil.

I desperately tried to find the source of the invasion and more importantly, looked for ways of getting rid of the bugs. Research identified the culprit as *Cordylobia anthropophaga,* also known as the mango fly, a horsefly common all over Africa; the crawling things that were eating me alive were the flies' larvae. The remedy that was suggested in the literature called for covering each infected site with Vaseline, applying downward pressure about half a centimeter either side of the boil, then bringing the pressure together trying to get under the maggot, and pushing it up and out. This was fine in theory, but in practice it proved an impossible task; there were just too many larvae, and often instead of getting a maggot to come out, I managed to have it burrow even further inside the skin.

The literature also said that after a few days—perhaps three to five—the larvae would burst out of the host, on their way to metamorphosing into pupae and ultimately becoming new flies. In my case, this did not happen. Apparently, these maggots were quite comfortable staying as such, inside my body, eating away, going deeper and deeper, until the superficial boils disappeared, leaving only bloody scars behind. But the damned creatures were not gone, but thoroughly ensconced in my flesh.

After a week of torture, I checked myself into a hospital and sought professional help in getting rid of the infection. The doctors, however, were as much at a loss on what to do as I was. I was put under anesthesia so they could make incisions on my body and find and remove the larvae. This was only partially successful, though, because some larvae had broken into internal organs—liver, kidneys, even my heart—and their removal could prove fatal. The doctors sewed me up, and upon awakening, presented me with the dire facts of the situation: I was going to die, and it was going to be a very slow and exceedingly painful process. They could prescribe painkillers and take other measures to keep me as comfortable as possible, but the end was inevitable and would happen sometime in the near future. I was doomed.

I waited in agony for the inevitable. As I did, I tried to resolve many questions that had bedeviled me since the parcel arrived. First, who was doing this to me? I contacted the Sisters of Mercy world headquarters and was advised that yes, they had several small congregations in Tanzania, in the regions of Mwanza, Geita, Tabora, Arusha, and Moshi, all of them in the north and central areas of the country. However, there was no presence by the Sisterhood in the region that housed the mining center. So the identity of the authors of the letters remained a mystery. And it was unclear whether they or their agents had in fact been responsible for delivering the parcel to my doorstep.

As urged by me and my partners, the government of Tanzania launched a desultory investigation of the matter. As expected, they came up with nothing. Parallel investigations by the police here in the city also drew blanks.

Even more inexplicable were the motives of the senders. Granted, the mining operation at Ngualla had not been a model of thoughtful environmental management, but it was by no means the cause of the poverty and disease that afflicted the surrounding region. Why punish us for what was a more global, and probably insoluble, set of problems?

Finally, and most puzzling and disheartening, was the discovery that I alone among the members of the limited partnership had received a deadly package this holiday season. The only explanation, and it was a slender one, was that I was the only unmarried partner and therefore more "expendable" than the rest, whose families stood to be affected. But was that fair?

As I grew weaker and was kept alive on painkillers and blood transfusions, I could only wonder at the arbitrariness of fate. People get run over by buses, die in terrorist attacks, or succumb to a variety of diseases, and in every instance, you can say that their deaths were random and arbitrary and therefore required no explanation other than just bad luck. But my death was not random; perhaps it was senseless, but it seemed to fulfill some dark purpose that I could not fathom and did not accept. And that made it all the more horrible.

I concluded that perhaps the worst crimes are those, like my murder, that are doomed to remain unexplained.

* * *

Two things brought me back from this lingering death-watch. A few days after doctors confirmed my inevitable demise, I received a call from John, the general partner. He perfunctorily bemoaned my fate, and then unveiled the purpose of the call: the partnership desired to buy back my share in the enterprise for a "generous amount." He expressed the fear that if I died with no known heirs, my assets, including my valuable share in the limited partnership, would escheat to the state, and who knew what the state would do with it—maybe even appoint an overseer that would create problems for the enterprise. I was never greatly concerned about what happened to my estate after my death and had not thought of writing a will; these days, my interest in the topic was essentially nil. However, out of politeness, I asked, "And what kind of a deal does the partnership have in mind for me?"

John replied that they were willing to buy my interest in cash, and then mentioned an amount so ridiculously low that for a moment I was rendered speechless. When I recovered enough to respond, all that I could manage to say was, "I can't believe you guys want to profit so shamelessly from my misfortune. You are like vultures ready to pound on the dying. Forget it." I slammed the receiver on its cradle and refused to answer John's repeated efforts to contact me by phone, letter, or electronic message. I would rather give my share to the state than to such a corrupt bunch of people.

My second jolt came somewhat later when I reviewed, as I routinely did, the postings on Facebook of the Tanzania Daily News, Dar es Salaam's leading English newspaper. Among typical stories on political scandals, sports upsets, and foreign investment news, there was an item that struck a chord with me. It was a news item to the effect that a biochemical lab financed by the rare earth mining partnership had reported new breakthroughs in the fight to eradicate the mango fly, a "dreaded scourge of animals and even humans throughout Africa," through "bioengineering methods that interfered with the fly's development." The online story provided no additional details.

The article prompted me to call John again. "I didn't know we sponsored biological research labs in Tanzania. How come I was never told?"

There was a long pause at the other end of the line. Finally, he replied, "Well, we started sponsoring the lab as a humanitarian gesture after the first of the Sisters of Mercy letters."

He was clearly lying; only months had passed since the arrival of the first letter, not enough time for the significant breakthrough cited in the article to have occurred. Plus, John himself had suggested that we ignore the Sisters' complaints.

He went on, "I made the decision not to let the other partners know until we had some tangible results to report, for fear of being accused of wasting company money on an unproductive charity. As it turns out, this has the potential of being a very profitable venture."

I realized that I was not going to get anywhere by trying to cross-examine John, so I decided to switch tactics. "Very well. Please give me the lab's contact information. I want to congratulate the staff and see if any of their research is applicable to my condition."

There was another hesitation, but he finally gave me the lab's address, telephone number, and email address.

Right after I hung up with John, I called the number in Chunya he had provided. The telephone rang a dozen times before switching to voicemail. I identified myself and left a curt message asking for the lab director to call me back as soon as they got the message. I followed up with an email explaining my condition and again asking to be called. No responses were ever made to my increasingly urgent calls and messages.

While I was awaiting a response from Tanzania, I decided to take a closer look at our general partner's personal history. Much of what was available focused on his academic course of studies, his MBA degree from Wharton, and his meteoric rise in the business world. However, after much digging, I came across a *Vanity Fair* interview in which he was asked about his earlier years. He described himself as an orphan who was taken in by the Sisters of Mercy and placed in an industrial school in Dundalk run by the sisters. Further research revealed that all the industrial schools run by the Sisters in Ireland were closed because of allegations, some confirmed, of corporal punishment, neglect of various kinds, and sexual abuse perpetrated by lay staff in the schools. John himself may have been the victim of the mistreatment attributable to the Sisters.

The *Vanity Fair* article was vague on when John left the institution or how he managed to come to America. The discussion shifted to his years in college during which he supported himself through a series of menial jobs. "Yes, life was always difficult for me, but I overcame all obstacles and was able to succeed by every mean possible," he said, and I could imagine the self-congratulatory note in his voice as he bragged.

It did not take long for me to form the suspicion, which soon became conviction, that my infection from a Tanzania-sourced plague was the result of a ploy to kill me off and acquire my interest in the partnership. It was unclear whether any of the other partners were involved, but surely John was the mastermind.

The incriminating evidence was only circumstantial, but a person in my condition was not about to let the wheels of justice grind so I chose to take immediate steps toward retribution. The first thing I did was research the eating habits of the *Cordylobia anthropophaga* larvae. I learned that they would eat the flesh of any animal, whether living or dead. So, I ordered a fair amount of ground beef and put it in the refrigerator.

The next step was trickier. I went to one of the doctors that had assisted me earlier on in the failed attempt to defeat the maggot invasion. I told him I knew it was not going to make any difference as to the final outcome, but I would feel better if he would surgically remove from my body as many of the larvae as he could. However, I did not want the larvae killed but placed in a plastic bag that I could take home and dispose of as I desired. The doctor gave me a dubious look but acceded to my request. Three hours later I was on my way home armed with a plastic bag containing about three dozen white, squirming maggots, some still bloody from the removal process. Upon arrival, I immediately took the ground meat from the refrigerator, went to the laundry room, set the meat on a mat above the dryer, inside a very fine mesh tent I had erected there, and carefully emptied the plastic bag on top of the meat. It may have been my imagination, but I thought I could hear the sucking sound of the little monsters as they inhaled the meat.

From that point on, I needed only to wait, which for a dying man becomes a difficult task. As anticipated, the maggots metamorphosed into pupae and then became flies that circled aimlessly within the tent. The flies lay hundreds and hundreds of eggs, most of which I collected and stored in the refrigerator. I let the rest hatch, become larvae, and repeat the process once again. In a few days, I had a bag brimming with tiny eggs, just waiting to be hatched.

I then opened my most recent purchase: a deep red velour robe, which screamed luxury and comfort. I liberally doused the eggs inside the pockets and liner of the robe, wrapped it in cellophane, placed it in a Neiman Marcus shopping bag, and added a card that read, in a delicate cursive hand, "For one who has everything – let Irish eyes smile!" I arranged for a delivery service to take the package to John's home and leave it on his doorstep.

When I called to confirm delivery, I was told that as the delivery person was leaving after sounding the buzzer, he saw a middle-aged lady pick up the package, read the card, frown, and then smile and disappear inside. John had a wife and three teenage children, two boys and a girl.

"In all wars, there are civilian casualties," I told myself as I put Judy Collins' *Wildflowers* CD on the stereo. Soon a contralto voice was filling the room with its evocative sound. The third song brought tears to my eyes.

DUMMIES

Dummy, dummy, go out now and fill your tummy.
- William Goldman

Jason finished making his four-year-old granddaughter Amy a dummy only a few days before she died of a fulminant childhood disease. He had taken great pride in his accomplishment, for he was retired from a career as CPA, and creating things with his hands other than spreadsheets was a daunting new experience.

It had not been all that difficult. He had gone to Goodwill and purchased a used girl's skirt and a blouse to go with it. It did not matter if the colors did not match—yellow polkadot blouse, argyle skirt of faded primary colors)—Jason knew little about fashion and cared even less.

He tucked the bottom hem of the blouse into the top of the skirt and used safety pins to hold them together. The arms and legs were blanket strips rolled into tubes, inserted into the clothing, and secured with adhesive tape. The chest and abdomen were filled with newspapers and plastic bags to give them shape. For the head, he had purchased a discarded plastic doll, twisted off the head, and attached it to the neck of the blouse with tape.

It was crude and flimsy, but it was little Amy's gift from grandpa, and she played with it constantly until she came down with her fatal infection. Upon her death, the dummy sat, forgotten, on top of the girl's dresser.

Other deaths then followed in quick succession, as snowflakes driven by a winter storm. First, his son Albert, Amy's father, was electrocuted in a freak workplace accident. Jason's daughter-in-law Marie, distraught by the death of her husband and daughter, overdosed on sleeping pills. Finally, Jason's wife Estelle, whose body had been weakened by diabetes, suffered a heart attack and died in a matter of hours.

The fatalities of course caught Jason unprepared; how could anyone be ready to lose, in just a few months, all members of his immediate family? He loved each one of them, even his daughter-in-law, and the tragedies pounded on him like hammer blows.

Two days after Estelle's funeral he was seized by a strange compulsion. He began making dummies, one for each member of his departed family, and added a couple of extras for good measure. In the end, he had a motley array of six dummies, which he positioned in a semicircle at the edge of the dinner table, facing him. Being dummies, however, they just sat there. They did nothing to assuage Jason's grief.

He became distracted, gave up on personal hygiene, and lived off fast food, which he washed down with bourbon and soda. Even though he always had the TV on, he kept the sound on mute and followed neither the news nor the games, and least of all the various inane shows he used to ridicule Estelle for watching.

As he munched tasteless French fries and drank big gulps of Old Crow, Jason would hold imaginary conversations with the dummies that stood for his relatives. He found himself voicing forgotten complaints or reminiscing good times. His wife and son were favorite targets of his tirades.

"Estelle, I'm running low on tee shirts because you were too busy nagging me to darn the holes in three of them, so I finally had to toss them out."

"Remember, Estelle, the time we went to Quebec and you got drunk on anisette? I kept telling you to watch out because the stuff is sweet but potent and will knock you out without warning. Did you pay attention? Noooo!"

"I'm no longer playing golf, Albert. Without you as a partner, it isn't so much fun anymore."

"Pro sports are a racket, son. Everyone is on the take."

He then conceived a demented idea: he would get the dummies to speak back to him.

He started reading. He read online, he borrowed books from the public library, ordered a number from rare booksellers. He was looking for an animation spell that he could use to revive the dummies.

Most of what he found was useless. There were a surprising number of quacks who promised to sell him infallible spells granting his desires for love, power, revenge, and many other goals. Those, he quickly learned to disregard. Then there were "spells" for gamers, intended for an apparently vast teenager and young adult audience. Tripe.

His only dim hope lay in old magical treatises. He bought half a dozen reprints of occult arts studies from the fifteenth and sixteenth centuries. Although more legitimate in purpose—indeed, written in obvious earnest by learned men from all corners of Europe—they proved, by and large, to be disappointingly shallow.

A historical account of witch hunts in Scotland proved the exception. The book contained detailed case studies of women who had been found guilty of practicing black magic and burned at the stake. It included, as an appendix, the texts of spells found in the possession of the witches.

One such spell was designed to temporarily bring to "life" objects that could be used as weapons or tools in the pursuit of the witches' purposes. Jason read the spell with difficulty, for it was written in archaic Elizabethan English, and cast variations of it at his dummies. Nothing happened.

That night, after three glasses of bourbon, Jason fell asleep with his head flat on the dining room table. Subconsciously, he was bothered by the uncomfortable position, but could not muster enough energy to get up and go to bed. He was chiding himself for his laziness when he thought he heard a tiny voice.

"Grandpa, you have stuff coming out of your mouth!"

It was surely a dream, but Jason half-opened his eyes and felt spittle drooling from his lips. He sat up from the table and ran the back of his hand over his mouth.

"That's better," observed the same voice.

Jason's transition to full alertness was instantaneous.

He looked around the empty apartment. No thieves or marauders there. He got up and stumbled his way to the refrigerator. He took out a plastic bottle of water and drew a big gulp, trying to clear his thoughts.

"Can I have some? I'm thirsty."

Jason started shaking as he turned around and fixed his attention on the dinner table. The first of his dummies, the one he had made as a present for his granddaughter, had inched forward from the semicircle and had the cloth stubs that served as its arms crossed around what would have been its throat.

Jason's first thought was, *I've gone off the deep end*. The second was, *The spell must have worked*.

He placed the bottle on the table, sat down, and continued to stare at the dummy with the polka-dot blouse, making sure he was not having a nightmare.

"Grandpa, please, I'm thirsty!" wheedled the dummy in a plaintive tone.

Jason allowed himself to be drawn into the impossible dialogue. "But baby, you have no mouth."

There was a ripping sound and an opening slit materialized in the plastic head of the dummy. "I sure do! Gimme some!"

I'm having a nightmare, Jason repeated to himself. All the same, he leaned forward, placed the lip of the bottle against the newly formed slit, and tilted it downward. Instantly, air bubbles formed in the bottle as the water was drawn out.

"Thank you, Grandpa. I feel better!"

"You're welcome, sweetie..." began Jason, and cut himself short.

He withdrew the bottle from the dummy's slit and lay it with some force on the table. *I have to wake up*. He started to rise.

Instantly, there was another voice, old and cranky, which

he instantly recognized. "Aren't you going to give *me* some?"

He did not need to look up to confirm that the querulous question came from a larger dummy, that he had clothed in dark rags to represent his wife, who favored black as slenderizing.

"Estelle, is that you?" he asked.

The dummy replied irritably, "Who else would it be, you *dummkopf*?"

Jason threw his arms up in despair. "Does everyone want water?"

There were yeses all around.

"I don't have enough bottled water. It will have to be tap." He went to the sink and filled a pitcher.

"Ugh" complained Amy's dummy, but drank the tepid water.

Jason went around the semicircle, pouring water onto the mouth openings of the dummies. He then sat down and addressed the group.

"Now, I know I'm either having a nightmare or hallucinating, but could somebody explain how six dummies all of a sudden sprang to life?"

The largest dummy, assembled in memory of his son Albert, spoke up. "We don't understand it ourselves. It seems that you did something that managed to bring us to life."

Marie, Albert's husband, piped in. "I read it online somewhere. Psychic energy can be channeled to bring inanimate objects to life."

"Poppycock," argued Estelle, always at odds with her daughter-in-law. "There has to be a better explanation than that."

"All right, all right," said Jason placatingly. "It is what it is. I'm enjoying having all of you around, however strange. Everybody okay?"

"For now," replied Albert. And that was that.

* * *

Jason's life changed very little following the reanimation of his dummies. He continued to eat poorly and drink heavily, and sometimes would not manage to make it to bed to sleep off his inebriation. Other nights, though, and often during the day, he would sit at the kitchen table and engage in disjointed conversations in which the four dummies representing his close relatives joined. Jason inquired as to who the silent dummies were and why they failed to speak. The Albert dummy shrugged his fabric shoulders and replied dismissively, "We don't know them, but we think they are supposed to be guardians."

"Guardians of what?"

The dummy shrugged again, impatiently. "Guard against whatever happens here. We don't know what they are supposed to ward against. Maybe they are here to make sure that we don't misbehave."

Noting his discomfort, Jason changed the subject. "I was watching the PGA tournament yesterday on the tube. You would have laughed with me. They are such amateurs these days. You and I could have done better than those clowns." And father and son got into an animated conversation about the days of Nicklaus and Palmer.

* * *

It was Amy's dummy who first brought up a new request. "Grandpa, I'm hungry."

Jason was already used to the dummies' bizarre anatomies—they "drank" water frequently, but water never seemed to leave their rag and paper bodies. But feeding them was a new level of strangeness. "But sweetie, you don't have a stomach. You couldn't digest food."

Estelle cut in. "Jason, stop confusing the child. Of course, we can't digest solid food. But liquids, that's something else."

Jason's eyes opened wide as new understanding came in. "You mean, like fruit juices? I have some orange and apple juices in the fridge. The apple juice is a little old, but the orange juice is fresh. I can get some…"

"No, silly," cut in his wife. "Juice is mostly sugar. Your granddaughter needs something more substantial, more nourishing."

"I get it. Liquid protein? I can go to the health food store and buy a few jars."

"No, no," replied Estelle, sounding exasperated. "She needs more complete nutrition: protein, vitamins, ions, glucose, lipids, minerals…"

"You got me now," replied Jason, upset at his wife. "Where can I get a diet supplement that has all of these things?"

Amy pleaded again, sounding ready to burst into tears. "I want blood!"

Jason whipped back at his granddaughter, astonished. "Blood?"

A chorus of loud voices rose from his creations. "*Blood!* We want *blood*!"

"That's impossible!" replied Jason, barely able to master a rising hysteria. "Where am I going to get blood for you guys?"

Estelle's tone became sarcastic. "You are the man of the house. You'll think of something."

* * *

Jason bought liver and kidneys at the Safeway and then found an Asian market where he got hearts and pig blood. He drained the blood from the organs and spooned the liquid to Amy and the other dummies. They did not protest but did not seem to enjoy the offerings as much as he had hoped.

He bought some prime rib and, before cooking it, squeezed the red liquid from the meat and gave some to Amy to try. The dummy's "mouth" puckered in disgust. "That's not blood."

Jason did a little internet research and found out that the "blood" in meat is really not blood, but something called myoglobin. He turned to his granddaughter's dummy, his patience exhausted. "You have very demanding taste, for a dummy. It's back to liver and kidneys!"

Marie, who usually kept quiet, came to her daughter's defense. "She's only a child and is tired of the stuff you are feeding her. The blood from store-bought organs is stale. She needs fresh blood."

"Fresh like how?" Jason almost did not ask the question, anticipating the response.

"Fresh like from a living creature."

"Do you mean I need to sacrifice a poor animal in order to feed you? No way!" Jason pounded on the table, his anger rising.

The dummy of his son Albert provided a reasonable-sounding explanation. "Look, let's give it a try and see if you are convinced. Make a cut on your little finger, squeeze some blood into a spoon, and give it to Amy. She'll tell you if that's what she wants."

"What if she likes it?" replied Jason, in a fury. "I'm not going to cut myself to pieces to feed a dummy!"

Albert remained rational. "At least we'll know if what Amy says she wants is what she really needs. Come on, Dad. Do it for us."

"You've never explained why all of a sudden you need blood, let alone fresh blood."

"Dad, I can't explain it. Each day we feel weaker, and something is telling us that if we don't get blood we'll die again."

"What do you mean by 'die again'? You are just paper wads and old clothes. You are not alive."

"If you really believe that, it's time for us to go."

Jason could think of a thousand reasons for refusing to go ahead with the test, and only one in favor: he felt he needed the company of his resurrected family and could not bear to contemplate returning to the way things were before Amy's dummy first spoke.

"All right, but we are creating more problems that we won't be able to solve." He dug in the kitchen drawer for the little paring knife, placed a tablespoon under his left hand, and made a diagonal cut across the fleshy part of his thumb. Grasping the thumb with his right hand, he squeezed a trickle of blood onto the spoon. He took the spoon to his granddaughter's dummy; the slit that served as mouth seemed to distend greedily to receive every drop of the blood.

Jason turned around and ran water on the wound, applied Neosporin to the surface of the finger, and wrapped it with a Band-Aid. As he returned to the table, he looked at his granddaughter's dummy.

"Grandpa, that was yummy! You have the bestest blood!" reacted the dummy.

"You are a bunch of frigging vampires!" exploded Jason.

Not surprisingly, Estelle had the final word. "Get used to it! There's a bit of vampire in all of us."

* * *

Jason made the rounds of all the pet shops in town, buying one or two hamsters in each. Killing each hamster filled him with guilt and revulsion; cutting each creature open to drain its blood into a pan was messy and smelly and disposing of the cadavers was a problem. He did not dare take them out with the regular garbage, for fear that the corpses would attract the neighborhood cats and raise suspicions. He ended up chopping each animal into little pieces, feeding the skin and tiny bones to the garbage disposal, and praying that the machine would keep working.

He discovered that a hamster had just enough blood for two skimpy servings for each dummy, with an extra helping for Amy. Luckily, the silent dummies turned down the blood offerings and remained aloof as the family dummies feasted.

He made do with the hamster supply for a couple of months but then got stuck again. He dared not go back to the pet stores. When the blood of the final hamster was apportioned among the dummies, he confronted them with the final choice he was about to make. "I'm sorry, folks. No more animals. No more blood. You'll have to learn to exist on the dry side."

There was a long silence, and then Albert remarked in a falsely cheerful voice, "But Dad, didn't we always want to get a dog, and Mom wouldn't let us? I bet she has changed her mind."

Estelle's slit of a mouth opened into a horrible smile. "Dogs? I *love* dogs."

* * *

Jason had trouble convincing the staff at the animal shelter that he would be a good father to a rescue dog entrusted to his care. "We prefer to release dogs to families. Single parents are a much higher risk, because you may fall sick or have something happen to you, leaving the dog alone. Plus, you are old, and you may not give the animal enough exercise."

After much pleading and promising on Jason's part, they agreed to let him take Audrey home with him. Audrey was a very old miniature poodle, with curly chocolate fur and liquid eyes. She was trusting and affectionate and took instantly to him. She was arthritic and nearly deaf, but she was docile and entered without hesitation into the cage in which she would travel to Jason's apartment.

"Audrey's owner was a widow that had to be taken to a nursing home," they told Jason. "Audrey has been well taken care of all her life, and we expect you'll treat her as well as her former owner did." Jason promised he would.

He was in such a rush to leave that he paid no attention to the final words of the lady at the desk: "We'll send someone on a home visit in two or three weeks to check on how the two of you are getting along."

Jason did not expect Audrey to be his companion for long, but all the same, he took her to a pet store and got her senior beef and rice canned dog food, dog treats, a rope and a couple of other toys, and a large water dish. Perhaps anticipating guilt, he spent a good deal of money trying to ensure that Audrey's final days would be pleasant and comfortable.

Jason and Audrey took to each other famously. The dog was always attached to the back of Jason's legs and followed him at every step he took. He would lead her on short walks around the neighborhood and feed her treats by hand. Audrey jumped into bed with him and slept curled against his body.

"Charming!" carped Estelle. "He brings food and ends up playing with it."

Jason decided that the love of a trusting beast was more important than the company of his family and, on the fifth night since the adoption he confronted the dummies.

"Listen, I've made up my mind. I'm keeping Audrey; you can do as you wish."

There was a heavy silence, which Marie finally broke. "I'm sorry to tell you this, but that dog has terminal cancer and will be dead in a few weeks."

Jason was suspicious. If the claim had come from Estelle, he would have disregarded it without another thought. Marie, however, had always been honest and forthright with him, and he doubted that she would start lying now that she was back as a dummy. "How do you know?"

"I can smell the corruption from here. Very soon she will start ignoring food, and her breathing will become labored. She will look disinterested in anything and finally grow still. I had a dog that went through that process years ago, and it was very painful for both of us."

Jason didn't know what to believe. True, Audrey had become rather placid, but he attributed this to her advanced age. Was he about to lose a pet the same way his family had been taken from him?

The following day Audrey was rather morose, barely touched her food and could not be enticed to play. Jason almost had to drag her out to get her to walk to the corner to pee. He was disheartened when he returned to the apartment.

"See, we told you so. You better let us have her blood before you lose us as well," insisted Estelle.

"I didn't know you could be so cruel," snapped Jason.

"You did know, you have just willed yourself to forget," replied the dummy sardonically.

* * *

He laid Audrey in the living room, resting on a blanket. Jason had given her a huge dose of Benadryl and had essentially forced her to fall asleep. The dog was unconscious; she occasionally stared at Jason with sorrowful, unseeing eyes. As Jason hovered over the animal, sharp knife in hand, the Albert dummy called out instructions.

"First, make a cut across the neck, severing the windpipe. That should kill her."

Jason raised a trembling hand and struck Audrey with great force. The dog yowled desperately and attempted to move, but it was too weak and submitted. Blood began pouring down its cut open neck, and Jason immediately placed a bowl under the head to capture the fluid. Audrey's body went into convulsions, which grew weaker after a few moments and finally ceased.

Tears blinded Jason, but he substituted another bowl for the almost full one. "Give her a cut below the groin, to capture blood from the lower part of the body," instructed Albert from above. Jason complied, his shoulders heaving with sorrow.

In the end, he harvested four bowlfuls of warm blood from the dead animal. Jason put the bowls in the refrigerator and went to the bathroom, where he vomited and bawled for several minutes. Then, composing himself, he wrapped Audrey's body in the blanket. He would take it to the park that night and bury it there, hopefully without being seen. But, right now, it was feeding time for the dummies.

* * *

Two weeks passed. Audrey's blood was gone, and the animal's carcass rested in peace under the leaves. But peace evaded Jason; he had nothing with which to feed the dummies and had flatly rejected the suggestion that he get another dog.

"You could never take care of your family," chided Estelle.

"Grandpa, I'm dying of hunger," whimpered Amy.

"Father, do what you need to do, but we'll be gone soon," advised Albert.

Marie just sighed, resignedly.

A great weariness enveloped Jason. He could not keep the dummies, nor could he go back to his dark solitude without them. He changed into his best clothes, took the six dummies to the bedroom, and lay in bed with them on both sides of his body. "I'll feed you, but you will have to help yourselves," he advised. He closed his eyes and recited a silent prayer, or perhaps a farewell. He then cut his throat with the same knife he had used to slay Audrey.

* * *

Two weeks later, an inspector from the animal shelter appeared at the door of Jason's apartment. She knocked repeatedly, and getting no answer, went down to the building super's apartment and asked that he open the door for her.

"We have been trying to contact him for days to arrange for a home visit for the dog he rescued. He never answered the phone or responded to our text messages and emails. Something is wrong."

The super was grumpy, but the lady had an air of authority and expressed her request firmly. He led her upstairs and opened the door of the apartment.

The lights were out and the air inside was close and had an unpleasant odor. The apartment was empty except for the corpse of a fully dressed old man, lying on the bed and as pale as the bedsheets. He exhibited a wide gash across the neck; blood had caked on the surface of the wound but was not visible anywhere else.

Everything was in order in the apartment, except for two oddly dressed dummies that were sprawled atop a bookcase, their heads resting on the wall. Around them, and on the floor beneath, were numerous rags, plastic bags, and discarded clothing, including a hideous yellow polka-dot blouse that once may have belonged to a child.

A Boon from an Angel

Azrael's hand is on your shoulder, Human.
I am here for your soul.
- S.G. Night

Norman first saw the angel on one of those November nights in which the temperature is too low for air conditioning but too high for the heating unit to do any good. Unable to sleep, he rose from his bed, perspiring, at that terrible hour of three a.m., when the light of day is but a distant hope. He sat for a moment, looking at the nightstand clock and debating whether to placate his bladder with a quick trip to the bathroom.

His throat was parched, and he felt wide awake. "I'll make myself some herbal tea and read a little. Maybe then I will be able to doze off," he thought. He walked over to the kitchen, filled the kettle, and turned on the gas. He placed a bag of chamomile tea in his mug and went to the bathroom to relieve himself while the water boiled.

He went back to the bedroom in search of the spy novel that had failed to lull him to sleep. Then he saw the angel.

She/he/it was floating above one of the pineapple-shaped finials of the brass footboard of his bed. It was transparent and shone with an inner light while pulsating with energy. It looked humanoid but somewhat shorter than a grown man. Its coal-black hair flowed erratically as if blown by an unseen wind. Its eyes had no whites and were bottomless cauldrons of flame.

Norman cowered, crouching a few steps from the bed.

"Do not fear. I mean you no harm. I am just making a courtesy call." Its voice was clear but lacked sharpness, like a melody played by a golden horn. The sound resonated throughout the chamber and terror amplified it in Norman's mind.

"What do you want from me?"

There was a silence, as if the visitor was considering how to best explain its appearance. "We come before your kind when we have important news or if one who is ailing summons us."

"But I have not asked for you."

"Maybe you do not realize it, but you just did so. Has anything of significance happened to you in the recent past?"

"Well, I was fired from my job with the insurance company a couple of days ago."

"Was that unexpected?"

"It surely was. I had worked for them for over forty years and had an excellent record, first as an agent, and later as a manager."

"Then why did they fire you?"

"They said they needed new blood in my district. I think they felt I was making too much money and they could replace me with someone younger at half the salary."

"And you feel this was unfair?"

"It was. And it hurts the most because I am now unemployable."

"So, what do you do with yourself these days?"

"Nothing much." Norman let out a bitter sigh.

The angel fluttered about as it readied the next question. "And how is your personal life?"

"What life?"

"Don't you get any joy from your wife and children?"

"My children have grown up and gone away. They remember me with a card on Father's Day, if I am lucky."

"And your wife?"

"My second wife divorced me not long ago and took everything. This ridiculous bed is all that is left of our marriage."

"You must have hobbies, things to fill your time."

"I used to play tennis passably well until my hip gave way and had to be replaced. Now I just barely limp around."

"Is there anything left that gives you pleasure?"

"No. Food no longer appeals to me. Television is a waste. I used to rent porno movies from the midnight store but those are silly—same people doing the same things the same way, over and over. Boring."

"You sound weary of life."

"I guess I am." Norman sighed again.

There was another silence. Then the angel asked, "If you were to be granted a boon—a gift from heaven—what would you want it to be?"

Norman did not hesitate. "I would wish to love and be loved, just for once. I have never experienced true love."

"That boon is not easily granted. To be loved, you must believe you are worthy of love, must behave in a way that inspires love, and most of all, you must love yourself. Can you accomplish these things?"

"I don't know. It seems too much bother at this point."

"You have a lot to do before you are ready for such a gift. I will return in a year and a day to check on you and determine if you then deserve the boon you seek." And the angel was no longer there.

Norman was at first too bewildered to react. He even debated whether the vision was true or a nightmare served up by his troubled mind. But every time he was assaulted by doubt, the memory of those crimson eyes reassured him. At last, ten days after the apparition, he began to carry out a plan of action.

First, he bought himself new clothes. Nothing fancy, but comfortable and new-looking. He got a fresh haircut and resolved to shave and tidy himself up every day. He joined a spa and started to get himself back in shape. He applied to every insurance company he knew, vying for positions that were beneath his experience and capabilities, and was able at last to land a job investigating and settling claims.

Suddenly he was busy and would return to his apartment rather tired. He was able to conquer insomnia and sleep through the night for the first time in years.

Everything was falling into place. Everything, that is, except the romantic side of his life. He was not a religious person but joined several church groups catering to widowed or divorced men and women seeking companionship. The people he met at these groups were as needy as he but considerably less interesting. The women, in particular, were all looking for someone to take care of them, and their efforts to woo bachelors like Norman were so transparent that, under other circumstances, they would have come across as charming rather than pitiful.

Norman next took himself to singles bars in search of better luck. The women he met there were too young and interested only in boys their same age, or on the prowl for a sugar daddy. After a couple of failed attempts, he gave up on the bar scene also.

Like many before and after him, Norman searched for a companion online. He signed up for sites that offered to match him with the woman of his dreams and went on dates with females of every description. Most were boring or too flawed to arouse his interest. The best of the prospects was Ursula, a bottle-blonde divorcee who was smart, outspoken, and willful. Norman's dating became an unending ping pong match, in which every serve by him was returned with a smash by Ursula, seeking to score a domination point. Their affair, if it could be called that, lasted only four weeks, at the end of which Ursula walked out accusing Norman of being a chauvinistic pig. Which of course was true, but was hardly relevant; in his estimation, chauvinistic pigs had as much a right to happiness as anyone else.

The spring was over and his next encounter with the angel was approaching. Norman became increasingly desperate, because try as he might, he had failed to demonstrate the worthiness for love that would merit the promised boon. Then he was invited to a cookout at the home of one of his bosses, to celebrate Memorial Day and the start of

summer. The party, held in the backyard of a suburban estate, was mobbed, and Norman found himself surrounded
by strangers who seemed to know each other and chatted
amiably while ignoring him. Norman was getting ready to
leave when he backed into a petite, middle-aged lady who
seemed as out of sorts as he.

Norman apologized for colliding with her, to which she
replied evenly, "Don't worry. This place is so crowded that
I have been afraid I would be run over by someone. You are
just that someone."

Norman was attracted by the lack of pretense of the
words and took a close look at her. She was probably in her
late forties, well but not expensively dressed, not particularly pretty but not ugly either. She had a professional,
lived-in air and looked at the crowd with undisguised
amusement. At once, he liked her a lot.

"It would be much more tolerable if I knew anyone here
other than Steve," he declared. "I work for him but don't
mingle with his friends."

Her response surprised him. "I came to this party as a
favor to his ex-wife, who asked me to keep an eye on their
daughter Ashley, who just turned eighteen and thinks she
has license to do as she pleases. You know the type." She
chuckled.

"And is Ashley behaving?"

"Well, see for yourself. She is on the other side of the
pool, getting totally plastered, in the company of frat boys
hoping to get in her panties. I don't know what her mother
expected me to do."

"A heavy responsibility has been laid on you," he responded with mock gravity. "I suggest we let Nature take
its course and try to enjoy ourselves." He clinked his beer
bottle against the glass of chardonnay she was holding and
declared, "I am Norman. Pleased to meet you."

"And I am Claire," she acknowledged. "Please to meet
you."

From that point on, the cookout became much less of a
waste. Norman and Claire got along famously and soon

were giving each other sanitized versions of their life histories. Claire was an interior decorator who had married a self-involved pro golfer and divorced him after a while. She had lived by herself for the last twenty-odd years and spent her time working and pursuing her passions: gardening, reading Victorian novels (and watching the BBC adaptations on PBS), and playing the recorder, at which she was proficient enough to give concerts as a member of local Renaissance and Baroque music ensembles.

They left the cookout after an hour or two of pleasant chatting. They exchanged telephone and e-mail information, and Norman vowed to call her so they could get together for coffee or a drink. When Norman returned to his bachelor pad, he found it more barren and unwelcoming than ever.

Events followed in quick succession. By the Fourth of July, Norman had moved in with Claire, and the couple was starting to discuss a more permanent arrangement. Then disaster struck. Claire began complaining of not feeling well and suffered from poor appetite, back pain, fatigue, and nausea. After a series of tests and hospital stays, she was finally diagnosed with advanced pancreatic cancer, the fastest and most lethal form of the disease. Norman saw Claire wither away as the cancer spread to other organs.

The inevitable conclusion took place as October ended. The neighborhood children who pounded on the door of his apartment on Halloween night got no response, for Norman was at Claire's home, where a hospice team was providing care and comfort to the terminally ill patient. The end came on the morning of November 2nd. Norman and Claire's romance had lasted barely four months.

The night the angel returned Norman was in his apartment, which was in great disarray. His mourning suit lay crumpled on an armchair, the white shirt and narrow black tie forgotten on the floor. Norman had never felt so exhausted in his life yet was unable to sleep as he convulsed with grief from time to time. He lay naked in bed, reliving the joys and indescribable pains of the last few months.

Finally, he forced himself up and walked over to the kitchen to fix himself a cup of herbal tea, although he was certain that all the tea in the world would not help him that night. He lay in bed for a few seconds, waiting for the water to boil, and then he saw the angel again.

He had almost forgotten about the apparition. Too much had happened since their first meeting, and he was not sure he had accomplished what was needed to satisfy the angel's demands.

"Greetings," rang the mellow words of the angel. "How has it been with you since last we met?"

Norman felt too weak to pour out the anger he felt and instead replied in a low hiss, "I did all that you asked. I tried to make myself worthy of love and, by God, I succeeded. Yes, I succeeded only too well. I behaved as if I were worthy of love and found such love for the first and only time in my life. I finally gained true love and it was snatched from me right away. So it was all for nothing. Go away."

"But I promised you a boon and you have made yourself worthy of it. Have you not?"

Reluctantly, Norman nodded in assent.

"Then, are you ready to receive your gift?"

"I have known love and experienced its loss. I need no boons from you."

"But you do. That feeling you experienced for another human is certainly an aspect of love, but not the greatest. You have yet to learn to surrender yourself to your beloved and have the two become one, not just for a moment, but for all eternity. Look at me; do you feel love for me?"

"For you? I have never thought about it. You are not real, and in any case, you are not human. I fear you and am in awe of you, but that is not love by any means."

"Perhaps. May I kiss you?"

"You may, but your kiss will give me no pleasure. All pleasure left me when Claire died."

"We shall see."

Norman found himself being embraced by an insubstantial body that touched him very faintly, the caress of a summer breeze. His lips made contact with something that felt both soft and very cold, like a mouthful of snow. He closed his eyes to better savor the intimacy. His nostrils inhaled a subtle perfume that filled his lungs with bliss and left him yearning for more. His entire body was suffused with the essence of this being that was bestowing upon him the greatest gift a human can receive: a taste of immortality.

"You never told me your name. What shall I call you, now that we have become one with each other?"

"Humans have called me many names. The most common one is Azrael, the angel of Death," said the angel, and kissed Norman again, and entered his body even more fully.

The silence of the night was broken by the insistent whistle of the tea kettle, which went on for a long, long time, and which Norman never heard.

ABOUT THE AUTHOR

Born in Cuba, Matias Travieso-Diaz migrated to the United States as a young man. He is a former engineer and attorney who, following retirement, redirected his efforts towards fiction writing. He lives with his daughter and two dogs in the Washington, D.C. area. He describes himself as an "Animal Farm's goat, Packers and Barça fan, and lover of opera, classical theater, jazz, Italian food, and vino."

He is the author of numerous short stories, over seventy of which have been published or accepted for publication in anthologies, magazines, blogs, audiobooks, and podcasts. This is his first published collection of his short stories. He's also written a novel, *The Taíno Women*, set in Cuba's early colonial period, and a novella, *Lázaro Serrano*, set in Havana in 1762.

THE NIGHTMARE CYCLE

LAWRENCE DAGSTINE

This book of nightmares will cycle on to where you'll remember them long after you've closed the book and placed it on the shelf.

AVAILABLE APRIL 25, 2023

Dark Owl Publishing
www.darkowlpublishing.com

THE DARK

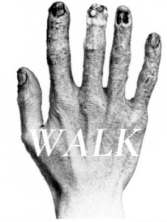

WALK

FORWARD

A HARROWING COLLECTION BY
JOHN S. MCFARLAND

Available in paperback and on Kindle from
DARK OWL PUBLISHING, LLC
www.darkowlpublishing.com

The Art of Ghost Writing

by

Alistair Rey

Short stories
from existences
beyond our own

Coming June 16, 2023
Dark Owl Publishing
www.darkowlpublishing.com

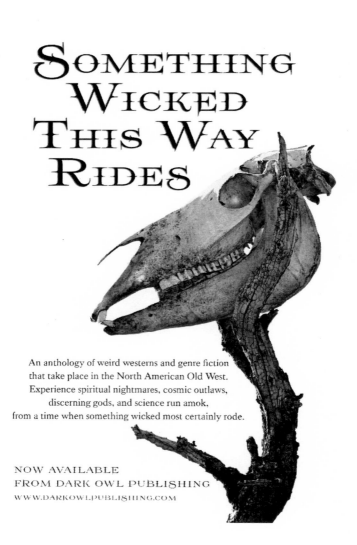

SOMETHING WICKED THIS WAY RIDES

An anthology of weird westerns and genre fiction
that take place in the North American Old West.
Experience spiritual nightmares, cosmic outlaws,
discerning gods, and science run amok,
from a time when something wicked most certainly rode.

NOW AVAILABLE
FROM DARK OWL PUBLISHING
WWW.DARKOWLPUBLISHING.COM